BBC Audio £8.99

D1347240

DEATH TO THE FRENCH

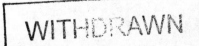

DEATH TO THE FRENCH

C. S. Forester

CHIVERS
THORNDIKE

This Large Print edition is published by BBC Audiobooks Ltd, Bath, England and by Thorndike Press, Waterville, Maine, USA.

Published in 2004 in the U.K. by arrangement with Orion.

Published in 2004 in the U.S. by arrangement with Harold Matson Co., Inc.

U.K. Hardcover   ISBN 0–7540–9915–6 (Chivers Large Print)
U.K. Softcover   ISBN 0–7540–9916–4 (Camden Large Print)
U.S. Softcover   ISBN 0–7862–6299–0 (General)

The text of this Large Print edition is unabridged.
Other aspects of the book may vary from the original edition.

Set in 16 pt. New Times Roman.

Printed in Great Britain on acid-free paper.

British Library Cataloguing in Publication Data available

Library of Congress Control Number: 2003116382

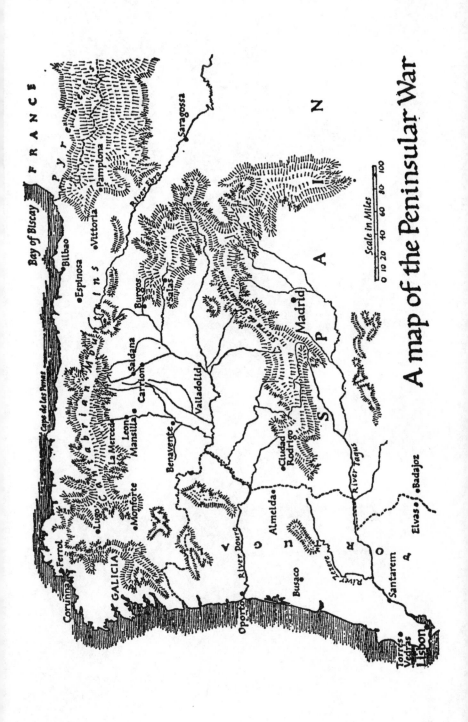

A map of the Peninsular War

CHAPTER ONE

Half a dozen horsemen were picking their way up a breakneck path. The leader of them was most conspicuous by the excellence of his mount, for his saddle fittings were severely plain and he wore a plain blue cape and coat and an unglazed cocked hat in sharp contrast with the scarlet coats and plumes of several of his followers. But when he pulled up at the brow of the hill and peered keenly forward across the tangled countryside some hint might be gained of the qualities which constituted him the leader. He had an air of authority and of composed self-reliance, and his blue eyes swept across the valley in a glance which noted its features instantly. The big, arrogant nose told the reason why the men in the ranks called him 'Conky' and 'The long-nosed beggar that beat the French', just as the hauteur of his expression explained why his subordinates alluded to him half ruefully, half deferentially, as 'The Peer'.

Drawn up below him was a column of scarlet-coated infantry, standing at ease; right ahead keen sight could discern little clusters and groups of men in green, mere dots on the landscape, sheltering behind trees and in dips in the ground. An occasional puff of smoke told that beyond the skirmishing line was the enemy. Lieutenant-General Lord Wellington hitched his sabretache on to his saddlebow, opened a notebook on it, and scribbled a few words on one of its pages, which he tore out. A scarlet-coated dragoon officer walked up his horse alongside as he did so, and took the folded sheet.

'For General Craufurd,' was all that was said to him.

The dragoon mechanically repeated 'For General Craufurd' and set his horse at the steep slope before them.

'Time for Craufurd to get back, Murray,' said Wellington. 'Now I want to see the columns across the river.'

He wheeled his horse and set spurs to him, and next moment they were clattering down the stony path again, sparks flying and accoutrements clashing as the rest of the staff tried to maintain the breakneck speed and headlong carelessness of danger which characterized the movements across country of the Commander-in-Chief. The dragoon officer would have a busy time trying to find his way back to his post of duty after delivering the order which sets this tale in motion.

A bugle was sounding out to the left.

'Fire and retire,' said a lieutenant to himself, listening to the high long-drawn notes. 'And not too soon, either. Where's that picket?'

He strode away along the top of the little

2

hill to look for it, with his crooked sword trailing at his side. To the conservative military eye his uniform was a ludicrous mixture. It was dark green instead of the scarlet which had won honour for itself on fifty battlefields; the black braid on it, the busby, the pelisse hung across the shoulders, all indicated, absurdly in an infantryman, an aping of Hussar equipment accentuated by the crooked sword. Yet it was only natural, because the Ninety-Fifth Foot were supposed to inherit some of the traditions set up by the Hussars when they were the most irregular of irregular horse. On the other hand the colour of the tunic, and the bugle horn badge, were no legacy from the Hussars—they recalled to the memory the fact that the first rifle regiments employed by the British Government had been recruited from the huntsmen of German princelings. Nevertheless no one now dreamed of sneering at this fantastic attire; the Ninety-Fifth Foot— the Rifle Brigade—had in the short ten years of its existence won itself a reputation worthy of the envy of any older unit.

'Fire and retire,' repeated the lieutenant to himself, as the bugle called again more insistently. There was a scattering rifle fire out to the left now, to endorse the urgency of the call. The dozen riflemen standing awaiting the lieutenant's decision on the top of the hill showed no signs of agitation. They knew their officer and trusted him, despite the fact that he was not yet nineteen years old. They had twice followed him across Spain, to Corunna and Talavera—to say nothing of the dreary marches of Walcheren—and they knew they could rely on him. The lieutenant shaded his eyes with his hand, but as he did so there was a clatter of equipment down in the valley and the missing picket came running up the hill.

'You're late, sergeant,' snapped the lieutenant.

'Yessir. We was nearly cut off and had to get round them,' explained the sergeant, and then, apologetically, 'Dodd's missing, sir.'

'Dodd's missing?'

'Yessir. I sent him forward and—'

'Do you know what happened to him?'

'No, sir. Didn't hear any shots fired out his way.'

The bugle rang out again amid a spatter of musketry.

'We can't wait for him,' said the lieutenant, with a decision acquired in a hundred rearguard actions. 'Sorry for him, but I expect he'll find his way back to us. Fall in, there. Left in file. Quick march.'

And the half company moved off, their rifles at the trail. The Ninety-Fifth were part of Craufurd's famous Light Division, whose boast was that they were always first into action and last out. Now they were covering the last stages of Wellington's retreat to the lines of Torres Vedras—the retreat during which they captured more prisoners than they left behind. But today they would have to report at least one 'missing'—Rifleman Matthew Dodd, cut off from his unit by the fortune of war.

CHAPTER TWO

Rifleman Matthew Dodd was already aware that he was cut off, although at the moment he was too occupied in saving his life to consider the consequences. He had been making his way back through the olive groves to his picket when he had heard strange voices ahead and had glimpsed strange uniforms. Bent double, and sweating under his pack, he had scurried through the undergrowth in the valley trying to make his way round the enemies who had interposed across his line of retreat. Half an hour of violent exertion had, he thought, brought him clear, when at that very moment a shout told him that he was observed by some other detachment. A musket rang out not far away from him and a bullet smacked into a tree-trunk a dozen yards away. He turned and ran again, uphill this time, in a direction which he knew took him away from his friends but which alone, as far as his skirmisher's instinct told him, was still not barred by the French advance guard. There were more shouts behind him and a crashing among the undergrowth which told him that he was closely pursued by a dozen men.

He dashed along up the steep slope, his pack leaping on his back, and his ammunition pouches pounding on his ribs. Soon he emerged from the olive grove on to an open, heather-covered hillside. There was nothing for it but to continue his flight without the protection of the friendly trees—either that, at least, or to turn back and surrender, and Dodd was not of the type which surrenders too easily. He ran heavily up the hill. Twenty seconds later the first of his pursuers reached the edge of the grove, and had him in clear view. They raised their muskets and fired at him, one after the other as they came up, but Dodd was a hundred yards away by now, and no one could hope to hit a man a hundred yards away with a musket, especially when panting from heavy exertion. Dodd heard the shots, but hardly one of the bullets came near enough for him to hear it. He climbed on up the steep slope until, when the last shot had been fired, he deemed it safe to spare a moment to glance back. Half a dozen Frenchmen were reloading their muskets; half a dozen more were starting up the hill after him. Dodd plunged forward again through the clinging heather.

The hill, like all the hills in Portugal, was steep and rocky and seemingly interminable, rising bleakly up from between two wooded valleys. He laboured up it, his steps growing slower and slower as the slope increased. Halfway up he stopped and looked back again.

The Frenchmen had ceased their pursuit and had drawn together to go back down to the road. Dodd's jaws clenched hard together. He threw himself down among the heather and pushed his rifle forward; an outcrop of rock provided a convenient rest. He cocked the rifle, saw to it that the priming was still in place, and then looked along the barrel. Although a musket might miss a house at a hundred yards, the rifle could be relied on to hit a group of men at twice that distance. He pressed the trigger, and the flint fell. The priming took fire—in dry weather not more than one shot in ten missed fire—and the rifle went off. Through the smoke he saw one of the Frenchmen down the slope lurch forward and fall, rolling down the incline a little way before he lay still.

A yell of rage went up from the Frenchmen and they turned to pursue him again, but Dodd leaped to his feet and ran once more up the slope. One or two ineffectual shots were fired after him, but they went wide. And after a hundred yards or so more the Frenchmen abandoned the pursuit again, and went back to where some of them were still stooping over the wounded man.

Dodd had taken his revenge for being chased off his best line of retreat. It was annoyance at this fact which had caused him to fire that parting shot, for in the Peninsular War casual shootings were not encouraged by high authority : the general commanding in chief had confidence in the persistence of the 'offensive spirit' among his men without any additional stimulus.

CHAPTER THREE

A dozen French soldiers were marching down a Portuguese by-road. They were a shabby enough group in appearance, for their blue uniforms had been badly dyed originally and now, after months of exposure to the weather, had changed colour in patches, greenish and whitish and reddish, here and there, and every coat was torn and darned in sundry places. Their shakos were dented and shapeless, and the cheap brass finery which adorned tunics and shakos was dull and dirty. Up to the knees their legs were white with dust, and their faces were grimed and bearded. Every man marched bent beneath a mountainous pack, round which was looped his greatcoat, and from which depended all sorts of curious bundles, varying with each individual save as regards one bundle, the most curious of them all. Each man carried one of these—eight hard flat cakes, irregularly square, strung on a cord, through holes in the middle, for all the world like monstrous Chinese coins. The likeness had been noted in the French army, and these cakes were always alluded to as 'cash'. Each weighed one pound, and represented one day's rations.

A French general considered he had done his duty by his men if he issued one pound of this flinty bread per head per day—anything else they needed he expected them to gain from the countryside. When the advance was resumed after the defeat at Busaco every man was given fourteen of these one-pound biscuits, and told to expect no further issue of rations until Lisbon was reached; from which it can be deduced that these men had been six days on the march from Busaco. Six days ahead of them lay the Lines of Torres Vedras, barring them eternally from Lisbon, but they did not know that. No one in the French army as yet knew of the existence of the Lines.

Sergeant Godinot was in command of the party, and the six men behind him were his particular friends, Boyel, Dubois, little Godron, and the others. Two hundred yards ahead marched the 'advance guard' of two men; two hundred yards behind came the 'rear guard', for although the detachment was marching in the midst of the French army precautions had to be taken against ambush, for in Portugal every man's hand was against them. Even when Godinot called a halt, and the exhausted men lay down to rest at the side of the road in the shade, one man was detailed to patrol round them.

'How much farther before we find this uncle of yours, sergeant?' asked Boyel.

Godinot had an uncle who was a general in Soult's army in the south; for eight hundred miles of marching the sergeant had been encouraging his section with descriptions of the golden times he and his friends would enjoy when they came under his command. Godinot shrugged his shoulders.

'Patience,' he said. 'We'll find him sooner or later, never fear. Have I not brought you safely so far?'

'You can call it safe, I suppose,' said little Godron. He was lying on his back with his legs in the air to relieve his aching feet. 'Marching, for six months. One good meal a week when we've been lucky. A battle once a month and a siege every Sunday.'

'There's gratitude,' said Godinot, grinning so that his white teeth flashed brilliantly in contrast with his sunburned face and black moustache. 'Who was it found that jeweller's shop when we took Astorga? Why, there are three gold watches ticking in your pack this very minute, you—you ungrateful viper. How you've kept them I don't know. That little Spanish girl at Rodrigo took all my loot from me. But we'll get some more before long. Just wait till we find my uncle. He's the chap for me.'

'Don't believe old Godinot's got an uncle,' said someone. 'He got us to join his regiment under false pretences.'

'And where would you be if I hadn't seen you at the depot and taken you under my wing?' demanded Godinot. 'Shivering in Poland or somewhere I expect, with no Daddy Godinot to wipe your nose for you. You blues don't know when you are well off.'

A 'blue' in the French army is a recruit— because until he grew used to it, the recruit went blue in the face under the constriction of the uniform stock.

'Why,' went on Godinot, 'perhaps—'

But Godinot's speech was interrupted by a loud challenge from the patrolling sentry, followed immediately by a shot. All of the detachment scrambled to their feet and grasped their muskets, following Godinot in his rush to where the sentry, his musket smoking in his hand, stood peering through the olives.

'A green Englishman,' said the sentry, pointing. 'That way.'

'After him!' said Godinot. Since the day of Busaco every one in the Eighth Corps knew what a green Englishman was.

The detachment began to struggle through the olive groves, crashing among the branches on the trail of the hurrying rifleman. Five minutes of hot pursuit brought them to the edge of the grove, where a high, bare hill mounted up in front of them. The dark-clad Englishman was toiling up the slope a hundred yards ahead. Godinot dropped on one knee, trying to calm his laboured breathing, and fired hastily, without result. The others as they came up pitched their muskets to their shoulders and pulled the trigger.

'Enough of that!' snapped Godinot. 'Reload. Come on, you others.'

He pressed on up the slope with half a dozen men beside him. But the Englishman had the longer legs or the stouter heart. At every stride he increased his distance from them.

'Oh, let him go!' said Godinot at length. 'The dragoons on the left will catch him.'

The men pulled up, panting.

'Come on back,' said Godinot. 'We'll never reach the battalion tonight at this rate.'

They began to plod down the hill again, leaving the Englishman to continue his climb up it. The incident meant little enough to them; every day for a month they had been accustomed to exchanging shots with English outposts. Yet even as they began to dismiss the incident from their memory it was sharply recalled to them. A shot rang out behind them, and Boyel pitched forward on his face, and rolled a little way down the hill, blood pouring from his throat. Everyone shouted with rage. Little Godron dropped on his knees beside

Boyel; the others, with one accord, turned to climb the hill once more in pursuit. A puff of smoke hung in the still air to show from whence the Englishman had taken aim. Yet as they set themselves to the climb the Englishman leaped once more to his feet and ran labouring up the hill, and five minutes more of pursuit told them how useless it was. They turned back again, to where Godron, with tears running down his cheeks, was kneeling with Boyel in his arms. An ounce of lead had torn a great hole in his neck and his tunic was already soaked with blood.

'Give my regards to your uncle, Godinot, when you see him,' said Boyel weakly. 'I shall not have the pleasure.'

And blood ran from Boyel's mouth and he died.

Godron was sobbing bitterly as Godinot knelt and made certain Boyel was dead.

'He has died for the Emperor,' said Godinot, rising.

'The first of us,' said Dubois bitterly. 'Six of us joined you, sergeant. Now we are five. Tomorrow—'

'Tomorrow it may be four,' agreed Godinot harshly. He was as moved as were the others, but he was in a position of authority, and had not so much time for sentiment. 'But we must join the battalion tonight, all the same.'

He was running his fingers deftly through the dead man's pockets and equipment.

13

'Money,' he said. 'Observe, eleven francs. You are witnesses. That is for the regimental funds. Cartridges. Here, divide these among you. Socks. Anybody want them? Well, they'll fit me. Nothing else of importance.'

He took the dead man's musket and walked across to a rock, where he smashed the stock and the lock with half a dozen blows.

'Take his bread, some of you,' he said. But the others hung back. 'Take his bread, I say. Dubois, Godron, you others. One biscuit each. Never waste bread on a campaign. Now come along back to the road.'

'But aren't we going to bury him, sergeant?' protested Dubois.

Godinot looked up at the sun to judge the time of day. 'There is no time to spare,' he said. 'We must join the battalion tonight. Come along, all of you.'

They obeyed reluctantly, trooping down the hill and through the olive groves to the road. They formed up and resumed their march, but of the six friends who had joined under Godinot's charge at the depot nine months before there were now only five, five men with heavy hearts and hanging heads. The sixth lay out on the bare hillside, where he would continue to lie all through the approaching winter, a noisome, festering mass until the carrion crows picked his bones clean to bleach in the sun and the rain.

CHAPTER FOUR

Rifleman Matthew Dodd went on up the hill. As soon as he was safe from immediate pursuit he sat down in the cover of a whin-bush to reload his rifle—reloading took so long that it was always advisable to do it in the first available moment of leisure, lest one should encounter danger calling for instant use of the rifle. He took a cartridge from his pouch and bit the bullet—a half-inch sphere of lead—out of the paper container. He poured the powder into the barrel, all save a pinch which went into the priming pan, whose cover he carefully replaced. He folded the empty cartridge into a wad, which he pushed down the barrel on top of the charge with the ramrod which he took from its socket along the barrel. Then he spat the bullet into the muzzle; it only fell down an inch or so, for it happened to be one of the more tightly-fitting bullets—extreme precision of manufacture was not demanded or considered necessary by those in authority. Since he could not coax the bullet down the rifling, he reached behind him to where a little mallet hung from his belt by a string through a hole in the handle. The fact that Dodd carried one of these tools proved that he was one of the careful ones of his regiment—it was not a service issue. Standing the rifle up on its butt

15

he rested the ramrod on the bullet and tapped sharply with the mallet; musket and ramrod were so long that only a tall man could do this easily. The blows of the mallet drove the bullet down the rifling until at last it rested safely on top of the wadding; then Dodd hung the mallet on his belt again and replaced the ramrod in its groove. After that he had only to make sure that the flint was in good condition, and then his rifle was ready to fire again. Dodd went through all these operations mechanically. Months and months of drill had been devoted to making him mechanically perfect in loading, so that he would not in a moment of excitement put the bullet in before the powder, or omit to prime, or fire the ramrod out along with the bullet, or make any other of the fifty mistakes to which recruits were prone.

It was only then that he had time to consider his position and think what he had to do. He settled down in the shelter of the whin-bush, easing his pack on his shoulders; three years' campaigning had taught him the importance of making the most of every moment of rest. Somewhere to the south of him was his regiment, which meant to him his home, his family, his honour and his future. To rejoin his regiment was the summit of his desires. But the regiment—so his extensive experience of rear-guard actions told him—had been marching hard in retreat for the last

16

two hours, while he had, perforce, been going in the opposite direction. The regiment was ten miles away by now, and between him and it was not merely the enemy's advance guard but probably a whole mass of other troops; the detachment which chased him would not have been moving isolated in the way he had found it if it had not been well behind the front line. Merely to follow his regiment would simply carry him into the arms of the enemy.

Military instinct called upon him to find a way round—that was the earliest tactical lesson the regiment had taught him, five years ago on the high Downs at Shorncliffe, with Sir John Moore on his white horse riding up and down to see that every recruit learned his part. South-east from him ran the Tagus, and along the Tagus bank he knew he would find a road which would take him to Lisbon and the Lines—he had tramped that road a dozen times already. To reach it he would have to get across the pursuing French army and pass forward round its flank. Dodd had never seen a map of Portugal in his life, and could not have read it if he had: he had learned his geography by experience. With his face up-turned to the sky he visualized from memory what he knew of a thousand square miles of country. He knew the two main roads by which the French were advancing. There was a chance—a faint chance—that he could reach the third road and find it unguarded. It would be one, two, three, four days' march with luck to the Tagus, and two—three, perhaps—to the Lines at Alhandra from the point where he would meet the river.

In his haversack there were two pounds of what the army termed 'bread'—unleavened biscuits only a shade better in quality than the French—and a beef-bone with some stringy meat still adherent. Dodd was a careful soldier; he had saved that meat from his last night's ration, knowing well that when on rearguard duty it was no unusual thing for camp to be pitched long after midnight, much too late for the wretched ration bullocks to be slaughtered and cut up and cooked. In the twin pouches on his belt there were fifty-five cartridges and a packet of flints—he felt to make sure. His rifle was loaded and his sword bayonet hung on his hip. He was as well equipped as a private soldier could hope to be. He wasted no time repining over the shortcomings of his outfit; he heaved himself to his feet, looked cautiously round him for signs of the enemy and, finding none, began to plod stubbornly south-eastwards through the heather. The hillside was bare and open, and there was no possible chance of concealing his movements for a mile or so.

But the rifle-green colour of his uniform was some slight protection, all the same; a scarlet infantryman—and nine-tenths of Wellington's army was scarlet infantry—would have been absurdly conspicuous. And his buttons and badges were black, with nothing to catch the sun and reveal his presence. The brave old Duke of York at the Horse Guards might not be very receptive of new ideas, but once he could be induced to accept an innovation he could be relied upon to see that it was carried out to its logical end. In the same way the long bayonet which tapped on Dodd's hip was really a short sword, because skirmishers and sharp-shooters might find their marksmanship impaired if they had to aim with a fixed bayonet, although at any moment they might be called upon to fight hand to hand. So to this day the Rifle Brigade flaunts its black buttons and badges, and 'fixes swords' when its fellow regiments 'fix bayonets', and carries its rifles at the 'trail' instead of at the 'slope'.

The dark green dot moved slowly along the hillside. At its end the hill sank in an abrupt shoulder, dropping down into a tortuous valley winding its way through a tangle of other hills, in which Dodd guessed he might find a rushing stream, and probably some sort of track, or possibly a real road—but that was not very likely, for roads were few in Portugal. He approached the sky-line cautiously, and when he reached it he sank down upon his face in the heather, hitching himself forward with his elbows to see what lay before him.

There was the little stream he had expected,

much contracted now at the end of summer and making its way tortuously among masses of boulders. But beside the stream there was a little house, walls and roof of grey stone, standing in the midst of a tiny field which generations of patient work had cleared of rocks and made fit for cultivation.

Houses spelt danger to an isolated straggler. Dodd lay long and patiently staring down at it. He could see no sign of life. There was no smoke, no movement. That was not specially surprising, because he knew that the country had been swept clean of inhabitants at Wellington's order. Food was to be all destroyed, women and old men and children were to be swept back into the Lines—Dodd had seen much of the pitiful processions during the retreat—while everyone who could handle pike or musket was to go up into the hills and feed as best he might while hoping for the chance of catching an isolated Frenchman.

So that the house should be empty of its owners was only to be expected; what was to be feared was that there might be Frenchmen there. Down in the courtyard, close by the grey stone wall which divided it from the field, was some whitish bundle—even Dodd's keen countryman's sight could not make out what it was. Probably an abandoned household bundle. At last Dodd decided that although he could see no sign of a Frenchman he had better not approach the house. He scanned the valley of the stream, noting the twisting path which followed it. By keeping to the hillside, above the sky-line, he could work his way safely to the next valley. There he could see a coppice, and he could go through that down to the little stream and reach the path unobtrusively. He hitched himself back above the ridge, peered round, and walked over the hill down towards the coppice.

Among the trees he moved with caution. He had the slope of the ground to indicate his direction to him, but that was a treacherous guide, as he well knew. And there might be enemies within ten yards of him. He peered round each beech trunk in turn as he came to it, looking for Frenchmen and planning his next advance. It was ironical that with all this elaborate caution he should have been taken by surprise. Something hit him on the shoulder. It was only a beech nut, but it made him leap as though it had been a bullet. Someone was peering at him through the yellowing leaves high up in a tree—he had forgotten to look upwards.

'P'st! P'st!' said whoever was there. '*Inglez*?'

'Yes,' said Dodd. '*Sim.*'

He could not raise his voice above a whisper, standing there in the silence of the trees. There came a scrambling among the branches. Two legs appeared dangling down, clothed in fantastic garments, fantastically ragged, half breeches, half trousers, with two

21

filthy feet emerging at the end. Their owner dropped lightly to the ground, and came towards him with a wreathing, dancing step, his swarthy face grimacing with triumph, presumably at having identified Dodd as an Englishman, despite his green uniform, by the caution of his movements. He was only a youth, and he was crazy.

He mouthed out a few halting words, but Dodd could make no reply. His knowledge of Portuguese was practically limited to the few words necessary to buy wine. The idiot took his hand and led him to the edge of the wood, pointing to the little grey house, only two hundred yards away. Again he spoke, and again Dodd could neither understand nor reply. The idiot seized Dodd's hand once more, and started to draw him along towards the house. He noticed Dodd's reluctance and guessed the reason for it. He spoke once more, and, seeing the uselessness of speech, he fell into pantomime. Shading his eyes with his hand, he peered round the countryside, and then made an emphatic negative gesture. Clearly he meant that the neighbourhood was clear of enemies. Dodd did not resist when the idiot drew him towards the house again.

Everything was very still. The sound of the little stream boiling over its boulders was all that could be heard as they approached the desolate little building. Inside the courtyard, beside the house door, Dodd halted abruptly.

A dead man lay there in a pool of blood. He was a very old man, white-haired, and his face was calm.

'*Sim, sim*,' said the idiot, pulling still at Dodd's hand. He led him behind the house.

The whitish mass which Dodd had observed there from the top of the hill was revealed now as a dead woman. Her grey hair was soaked with blood, and her open hands were lacerated as though they had been cut when she seized the weapon which destroyed her. Her ragged clothes were bundled up round her breast, and she lay there in pitiful nakedness.

The little group made a striking picture there beside the house at the foot of the hills—the tall, burly soldier in his green uniform, the idiot mopping and mowing beside him, and at his feet the naked corpse. Dodd stood there in silence, until the idiot broke into his sombre reverie.

'*Morran os Franceses!*' said the idiot suddenly.

Death to the French! That was the cry which was echoing through Portugal at that moment. He must have heard it often enough.

Dodd started out of his black mood. He made to go out of the courtyard, but, struck with a sudden thought, he stooped, and with a rough tenderness he pulled down the bloody clothes about the dead woman, and he folded the lacerated hands upon the breast. Then he turned to go, with the idiot beside him. The courtyard beside the house was littered with the little belongings of the dead couple.

Dodd had seen looted cottages often enough before, but this particular sight moved him inexpressibly.

'*Cavalheiros*,' said the idiot. He pointed to signs on the track indicating that horses had stood there beside the courtyard gate.

Dodd nodded; this was not the first time he had seen the handiwork of the French dragoons. The idiot pointed to the gate, went through the pantomime of mounting a horse and then of riding. Then he pointed along the track and down towards the hills away from the little wood of their first encounter. Dodd was glad of the information. He knew cavalry must be somewhere about. At the point where he had been cut off from his regiment the country had been so tangled that rear guard and advance guard had been composed of infantry, but out on the flanks the cavalry were fulfilling their usual role of screen. The fact that he had come into their zone indicated that he had made some progress towards his goal.

'Well!' said Dodd, with finality. He could do nothing here; it was his duty to push on. He pointed south-eastwards. 'Tagus?' he said interrogatively, and then, remembering the native name of the river, '*Tejo*?'

The aspirated 'j' was a stumbling-block, but he thought he had pronounced the name recognizably. Yet no sign of recognition came

24

into the idiot's face.

'*Tejo?*' said Dodd again.

The idiot muttered something, which Dodd strongly suspected not to be even Portuguese, but gibberish. Dodd could do no more. He turned away and began to tramp along the rough track beside the stream. A second later the idiot came pattering after him. They left the desolate house behind, with its deserted corpses, and walked on down the valley—the English soldier and the capering idiot.

When they emerged from the woods of beech and cork oak the sun was low on the horizon. Dodd began to think about making preparations for the night. He was not the man to risk losing his way by walking in darkness. In the essence of things he must sleep where no man was likely to come near, which meant, of course, sleeping on an open hillside. He could have no fire, for that would attract attention. Lastly, he must drink—the iron discipline of the Light Division had accustomed him to dispense almost entirely with water during the heat of the day, but at the same time had given him the habit of drinking immense quantities at nightfall.

His simple demands were readily fulfilled. The stream was beside him, and he knelt to drink. He emptied his water-bottle—'canteen' was its army name in these days—of its lukewarm contents, filled it, and drank, filled it again, and drank again, filled it again, and looped the strap over his head once more. The idiot beside him drank without so much formality. With his toes on the bank he rested his hands on two boulders protruding above the surface in mid-stream, and, lowering his mouth to the water, he drank great gulps as it flowed past his nose. Dodd was reminded of a chapter in the Bible he had heard read in church during his ploughboy days, about some old general who had picked his men for some special enterprise by the curiously arbitrary method of selecting those who lapped at a stream instead of drinking from their hands.

Darkness was now falling rapidly. There was a towering bare hill to their left and, leaving the path, Dodd set his face to it. Nearly at the summit was a little cluster of whin-bushes, and of these Dodd selected the easterly side. They would give him a little shelter during the night if the west wind brought rain. He slipped his arms out of his equipment, and unrolled his greatcoat, which he put on. Then he harnessed himself again with his pack, so as to be ready for instant action if an alarm should come during the darkness. The idiot had watched all these actions attentively, and when Dodd pulled out his bread and his beef-bone from his haversack he crept nearer in the twilight and held out his hands in supplicatory fashion.

Dodd was torn between two emotions. He wanted to feed the starving creature, and yet he had only two days' food to carry him through the ten days of marching which lay between him and his regiment. Duty told him to conserve his rations, pity told him to give. He hardened his heart and munched stolidly, ignoring the pitiful appeal. The biscuit was terribly hard, the beef was terribly tough. As a matter of fact the ox which supplied it had been driven one or two hundred miles on woefully poor food before it had been slaughtered; it had been cut up and subjected to the ill-directed attentions of the regimental cooks as soon as the breath was out of its body, being boiled in a cauldron for an hour or so, the longest that the fierce appetites of the men last evening could wait. But Dodd had known little better food during his five years in the army, and before that he had been the eleventh child of a farm-labourer earning ten shillings a week and had fed even worse, so that he bit into the tough fibres with contentment.

Yet when he began carefully to pack the remainder away in his haversack the idiot uttered a low wail of despair. He thrust forward his hands, he made pleading noises, and withal so gently and so movingly that Dodd could not resist his appeal. Cursing himself for a helpless fool, he broke a lump from a biscuit and thrust it and the remains of the beef into the idiot's hands. The pleading noises changed to sounds of delight. It was quite dark now, but Dodd heard the biscuit being crunched between the idiot's teeth. From the quality of the sounds he even suspected that the rib of beef was receiving the same treatment.

He sat huddled in his greatcoat for a few minutes, brooding over the day's events before going to sleep, when the sight of a glow in the sky far off brought him to his feet again. He seized his rifle and strode over to the edge of the hill, and the light was explained. Across the valley, stretching to right and left as far as the eye could see, were rows and rows of twinkling points of fire—the bivouac fires of an army. It was a sight he had seen often enough before; looking down at the irregular pattern, he could make a rough guess at the strength of the force encamped there; he could even, by noticing the size of the patches of darkness which broke the continuity, guess at the extent of the horse-lines and consequently estimate the proportion of cavalry and artillery. He did not trouble to do this. He had no report to make to an officer, nor would have for days; for it was of no consequence to him if twenty thousand or forty thousand men were there. It was sufficient for him to know that these must be the main column of the French left wing, across whose line of march or behind whose rear he must pass next day. They were five miles away, and it was scarcely possible that their outposts would trouble him here on his bare hillside.

He went back to his bushes, with the idiot rustling through the heather beside him. Loosening his equipment belt a couple of holes, he hitched his pack up under his back until it made a pillow under the back of his neck. He saw to it that his greatcoat was over his legs, and prepared to go to sleep, his face upturned to the stars which glowed brilliantly overhead—far more brightly than ever they did in misty England. A little wind was blowing, very gently, but he was in the lee of the bushes and it did not chill him much. Somewhere near him the idiot seemed to be flattening out a nest for himself in the heather, like a cat, and muttering to himself in monosyllables.

As Dodd was dropping off to sleep there passed through his mind another fragment of what he had once heard in church—something about birds having nests and beasts holes, while the Son of Man had nowhere to rest his head. Dodd did not realize it, but that quotation passed through his mind every time he composed himself to sleep in a bivouac. It was indicative of the fact that he would be asleep in two minutes' time—and, sure enough, he was.

Even now it was only eight o'clock in the evening. Dodd was merely giving a demonstration of that ability to sleep at any hour which has characterized the English private soldier, and has been remarked upon by diarists from generation to generation, from the time of Marlborough's wars to the present day.

CHAPTER FIVE

At intervals during the night Dodd stirred and shifted his attitude. He was still fast asleep, but if at those times there had been the slightest suspicious noise near him he would have been broad awake on the instant. But nothing came to disturb him. The shrieking of owls and the barking of a fox were natural noises which the mechanism of his brain filtered out and did not permit to interfere with his sleep. He was a veteran soldier.

He woke easily when the first suspicion of daylight came to lessen the pitch darkness of the night. There was a light rain falling; the coarse frieze of his greatcoat was spangled and silvered with it. He sat up a little stiffly, and looked round him. The idiot sprang into wakefulness when he moved, but beyond that there was no sign of life. He walked to the brow of the hill, but the fine rain drifting across the valley limited the range of vision so that nothing could be seen.

He made his preparations for the day. First he changed the powder in the pan of his rifle, sheltering it under his bowed body as he did so. Then, standing the weapon carefully against a bush, he unbuckled the straps of his pantaloons and drew off his shoes and stockings. There was another pair of stockings, worsted ones, in his pack, and he put these on after he had bathed his feet in the wet heather, being careful to put on his left foot the stocking which he had worn two days before on his right. He put on his shoes and buckled his straps again, ate a mouthful of biscuit and swallowed a mouthful of water, and he was ready for another twelve hours of marching. Grudgingly he tossed a fragment of biscuit to the idiot, who gulped it like a wolf. The poor wretch was shivering and stiff with cold.

Dodd started across the hill. From the ridge, as far as the rain would permit, he made a mental note of the lie of the country and its inconsequent tangle of hills, comparing it with what he had seen of the bivouac fires of the night before. It would be a dangerous march today, across the rear of the advancing column. He might encounter foraging parties or marauders or stragglers as well as units on the march. Beyond the road there would be the cavalry of the wings to reckon with. Within the next two hours he might be dead or a prisoner, and captivity or death would be imminent all through the day. But at present he was alive and at liberty, and, soldier fashion, he did not allow the other possibility to depress his spirits.

31

The rain grew heavier as he plodded on. The legs of his trousers were soaked with wet before very long and, although his greatcoat kept it out admirably, little trickles of moisture began to run down his neck down inside his clothes and cause him a good deal of discomfort. The wretched idiot at his side was soon whimpering with distress; Dodd, as he walked along, tried not to think what the rocks and boulders which they sometimes had to cross as they continued along the hill-tops were doing to the poor devil's naked feet. After all, as he told himself, he had not asked him to attach himself to him.

After two hours of difficult going Dodd grew more and more cautious. He must soon be nearing the high road. He strained his eyes through the driving rain to catch a glimpse of it, but the rain was too heavy to allow him to do so. The one element of comfort in the situation was that the wind was coming from the north-west, as nearly as he could judge, so that by keeping his back to it he not merely was preserving his direction but was also walking as comfortably as the comfortless conditions allowed. They came to a stream. Already, in that rocky country, the rain had swelled its volume and, it was boiling among the boulders. As Dodd splashed across it, holding up the skirts of his great-coat and wet to the middle of his thighs, he realized that a continuance of the rain would seriously limit his power of moving across country because of the deepening of the streams. And this one ran south-westward—he still had not yet crossed the main watershed between the sea and the Tagus.

Above the stream rose yet another precipitous slope, up which Dodd set himself doggedly to plod. The wind was working up to gale force, and the rain was whirling across the country with the torrential violence which can only be realized by those who have witnessed an autumnal storm in the Peninsula. The top of this hill was rounded instead of scarped; Dodd had to toil across it for some distance before the next valley opened up before him. What he saw there, dimly through the rain, caused him to drop hastily to the ground.

The high road crossed the valley diagonally before him, from his left rear to his right front, mounting the steep incline with a contempt for gradients which made one wonder at the boldness of the engineers, and it was crammed with men and animals and vehicles. Apparently it was by this leftmost road that the main train of the French army was being directed. Dodd's arrival synchronized with the disappearance of the last of the marching troops and the beginning of the interminable mass of impedimenta which an army of a hundred thousand men must drag behind it. Dodd lay in the heather while the rain poured down upon him, watching the march of the column, while the idiot whimpered at his side. Even an idiot could appreciate the necessity of lying still when French troops were at hand.

As far back as Dodd could see, and doubtless for miles beyond that, the road was jammed with wheel traffic. There were fifty guns and fifty caissons, there were the heavy wagons of the train, there were hundreds of country carts—the most primitive vehicle invented; each consisted of a long stout pole upon which was bolted a clumsy box-like framework of solid wood, much broader at the top than at the bottom. The wheels were solid, and immovable upon their axles, which rotated stiffly in sockets on the pole to the accompaniment of a most dolorous squeaking. Each cart was drawn by eight oxen, yoked two by two, goaded along by sulky Spanish or Portuguese renegades, and in each cart lay three or four sick or wounded Frenchmen, jolted about on the stony path, exposed to the rain, dying in dozens daily. Yet their lot, even so, was better than if they had been left behind to the mercy of Portuguese peasants.

Guns and wagons and carts were all of them short of draught animals—Dodd could see that nearly every gun had only five horses instead of six. And the hill they had to climb while Dodd watched was far too much for their failing strength. Only a few yards up the slope each vehicle came to a stop despite the shouts of the drivers. Then a team had to be unhitched and brought to reinforce the overworked animals. Then with whips cracking and drivers yelling the horses would plunge up the hill a little farther until some stone of more inconvenient size and shape than usual baulked their progress and the men would have to throw themselves upon the drag ropes and tug and strain until the obstacle was negotiated and a few more yards of the hill were climbed. And so on, and so on, until at last the top of the hill was reached and the vehicle could be left there while the doubled team descended to drag up the next; hours of agonizing effort, stupefied by hunger and rain and wind—a dozen such hills a day, and a hopeless future ahead of dozens more of such days.

Dodd could only lie where he was and wait for the slow procession to crawl past him. He wanted to reach the other side of the road; if he went back up the road to pass the rear of the column more quickly he would only have to retrace his steps once he was across. So he lay there with the rain beating upon him and the wind shrieking overhead; soon he was soaked to the skin, but still he lay, with the inexhaustible, terrible patience acquired in years of campaigning.

It was late afternoon before the last of the vehicles passed out of sight over the hill; it was followed by a mass of sick and wounded men on foot, staggering along blindly over the stony road, and after them came a battalion of infantry in rear-guard formation. Yet even when the rear-guard had disappeared Dodd still waited for fear lest stragglers and marauders should be coming behind. There were none, however. The French did not straggle to the rear nowadays, when they knew that the Portuguese who followed them up had a habit of roasting their prisoners alive, or boiling them, or sawing them in half.

Just before twilight came Dodd was able to descend to the road, and cross it, and mount the hill the other side. The rain had ceased now, but the wind was backing round to the north and blowing colder every minute. He was glad of the chance of exercising his shivering limbs—the idiot who still came with him was so cramped with cold that he fell down every few yards and shambled on all fours until he could rise to his feet again.

Bitter cold it was, but the wind and the exercise did at least have the effect of drying their clothes. Dodd plunged on through the gathering darkness, bent upon putting as much distance between him and the road as was possible before nightfall. He thought of the men of his regiment, gathering round roaring fires, with, if they were lucky, roast pork or boiled beef for supper, and perhaps a nip of brandy. There would be no fire for him tonight, as near to the French as he was, and there would be little enough supper.

It was on an open hillside again that Dodd stopped for the night. He would not camp in a valley or in a wood—that was the sort of place patrols would explore. Philosophically he chose once more the lee of an isolated patch of bushes, but there was comfort to be found in the sight of the glow of the French bivouac fires behind him this evening. With any luck there would be a clear road before him tomorrow back to the Lines—back to his regiment. Strangely, the idiot wanted no supper that night. Dodd could hear his teeth chattering where he lay some distance off.

And in the morning, before it was yet light, it was the idiot who woke Dodd. He was calling out in a loud voice, so that even as Dodd awoke and got to his feet his hand went out to his rifle and he stared through the twilight for an approaching enemy. He could see nothing; he could hear nothing save the idiot's voice, and as he went towards him the voice rose an octave and broke into laughter. Dodd knelt beside him; there was just enough light for him to see that the idiot was lying on his back with his arms thrashing about while he laughed and laughed. Then the laughter changed to words—terror-laden words obviously—while he struggled up to a sitting position and then fell back again. The poor wretch was delirious and in the grip of pneumonia—'fever', Dodd called it to himself. Dodd had to decide what to do; he made his decision in the course of his preparation for the day's march.

If he stayed by the idiot they would starve together. If he burdened himself with his weight he would never catch up on the marching French, never rejoin his regiment. All he could do was to leave him there, to starve if the fever did not kill him first. He made a pitifully feeble attempt to make the idiot comfortable among the heather, and then, sick at heart but fierce with resolution, he turned away and left him, chuckling anew at some comic thought which had penetrated his fevered, idiot's mind. The last Dodd heard of him was a new shout of *'Morran os Franceses'*—a fitting cry enough. Dodd left him there, shouting and laughing, to sink into exhaustion and coma and die, alone on the windswept hill. After all, a soldier had much more important work to do than to ease an idiot's last hours, as anyone would agree who did not have to make the decision.

CHAPTER SIX

Dodd had promised himself that he would not continue across country after noon that day. By that time he ought to be fairly safe from patrols, and would take the first crossroad that bore in approximately the direction he wished.

Before the morning was half over he came across a tempting path which he resolutely kept away from. Twice he saw grey villages in the distance and went cautiously round them out of sight; there was smoke rising from one of them, but smoke might at that point indicate the presence of French as much as Portuguese. He found a stream—a raging torrent after yesterday's rain—which gave him fresh heart because it was running in the right direction, towards the Tagus and not towards the sea. He marched on, never slackening his pace. A man who had marched with Craufurd to Talavera could do without rest. In the nearly roadless desert of the Lisbon Peninsula it was easy enough to keep straight across country, avoiding all the habitations of man. He kept to the hills, away from the sky-line, as much as possible, only descending into the valleys when his route compelled him to do so, and hastening across them with extreme care. All through that morning's march he saw no one, no man working in the fields, not a cow nor a sheep, nothing save a herd of wild swine in a beech wood.

That was only to be expected, for it was by Wellington's orders that the country had been swept clear of every living thing before the advance of the French. The crops were to be destroyed, the fields laid waste, the villages left deserted. An enemy who relied for his food on what could be gleaned from the countryside was to be taught a lesson in war. And the ruin and desolation caused thereby might even constitute a shining example to a later generation, which, with the additional advantages of poison gases and high explosive, might worthily attempt to emulate it.

Dodd indulged in no highfalutin meditations upon the waste and destruction. He had been a soldier from the age of seventeen. His business was solely concerned with killing Frenchmen (or Russians or Germans as the ebb and flow of high politics might decide) while remaining alive as long as possible himself. If by ingenious strategy the French could be lured into starving themselves to death instead of presenting themselves as targets for his rifle so much the better. It increased his respect for 'Conky Atty'—'Long-nosed Arthur', Viscount Wellington, in other words—but roused no other emotion. And as a last word in the argument it was only Portuguese whose farms were being burnt and whose fields were being laid waste, and Dodd had enough insular pride to consider Portuguese as not quite human, even now, although Portuguese battalions were now considered worthy of inclusion even in the ranks of the Light Division, and had fought worthily alongside the Ninety Fifth at Busaco and the Coa and the other battles to which he looked back with pride.

Somewhere right ahead of him came a

spatter of musketry fire, and Dodd's nerves tautened. Fighting indicated the presence of both enemies and friends. He pushed on cautiously, with his rifle ready for instant action. His instincts took him to the highest ground in sight, whence he might have an opportunity of discovering the military situation. He was throbbing with hope that perhaps there were English soldiers there. It seemed almost impossible, but there was a chance that he had wandered somehow into a rear-guard action.

The hill below him fell away into a steep, rocky precipice—the gorge of the rushing stream which coursed along its foot with a rough track running along its banks. The firing had nearly ceased now—Dodd could only hear very occasional shots and they were a long way away. Then, out of sight to his right, where the track turned round a shoulder of the hill, he heard the rapid staccato of the hoof-beats of a horse, galloping as hard as he could be driven along the stony path. Round the corner there appeared, far below him, the little figure of a man on foot, running faster than ever Dodd had seen a man run before, and twenty yards behind him came a French dragoon, his sabre flashing as he swung it in the air, leaning forward over his saddle as he spurred his horse in mad pursuit.

For a moment Dodd wondered why the man on foot did not have the sense to take to the hillside where the horseman could not follow him; he decided that he must have lost his head with fright, and pushed forward his rifle to stop the pursuit. It was a Frenchman he was aiming at; he was sure of that—he had aimed at French dragoons often before. He recognized the bell-shaped shako, and the horse's tail was undocked, in the French fashion. He cocked his rifle, aimed, and pulled the trigger. But it was incredibly difficult to hit a man at full gallop two hundred yards away with that rifle. Dodd must have missed, for the dragoon continued without a check. Then, while Dodd was frantically reloading, the Frenchman caught up with the man on foot. The sabre flashed again as he swung it round, slashing like a boy with a stick at a nettle. The man on foot staggered, with his arms round his head, but he fell beneath a second slash. The dragoon slashed again at his writhing body, leaning sideways off his horse to do so; he stabbed at it, and then, wheeling his horse around, he spurred it and reined it back until he forced the reluctant animal to trample on his victim, over and over again. Then he trotted back, his whole bearing full of conscious triumph.

Still Dodd had not contrived to coax a fresh bullet down his rifle barrel. He was cursing vilely at the weapon, for he saw dearly there would be no chance of a second shot. Then, when the dragoon was about to turn the corner, a ragged volley sounded from the other side of the gorge. The horse plunged and fell, pitching the dragoon over his head, and instantly a little group of men came leaping down the opposite hillside, splashed across the stream, and seized him just as he was sitting up, dazed. There appeared to be a brief consultation round the prisoner, and then the group, dragging him with them, mounted the side of the gorge almost to where Dodd lay watching.

They were Portuguese peasants, he could see—friends, that was to say. He walked along the crest to where they were gathered round the helpless dragoon. At sight of him they seized their weapons and rushed towards him. Some of them had pikes, two or three of them had muskets, one of them with a bayonet fixed, and apparently with every intention of using it.

'*Inglez,*' said Dodd hastily, as they came running up—that green uniform of his made this explanation necessary. The Portuguese always expected to find an Englishman in a red coat.

They looked their unbelief until their leader pushed past them and inspected him.

'*Sim, Inglez,*' he decided, and turned to pour out a torrent of rapid explanation to his followers.

Then he turned back to Dodd and said something which Dodd could not understand. He repeated the phrase, and then, seeing that it meant nothing to Dodd, he reached forward and shook Dodd's rifle.

'*Espingarda raiada,*' he repeated impatiently.

'Rifle,' said Dodd.

'Rye-full,' said the other. '*Sim, sim, espingarda raiada.*'

To his friends he repeated the word along with more explanation and a vivid bit of pantomime illustrating the rotation of a rifle bullet in flight. Clearly he was a Portuguese of more than average intelligence.

The party drifted back to where the wretched dragoon lay among the rocks, his hands behind his back and a cord round his ankles. His face lit up with hope when he caught sight of Dodd's uniform. The Portuguese leader kicked him in the face as he came up, and then, as he fell back among the stones, kicked him in the belly so that he moaned and doubled up in agony. That was enormously amusing; all the Portuguese hooted with joy as he writhed, and when he turned over on his stomach one of them stuck the point of his pike into the seat of his breeches so that he cried out again with pain and writhed over again on to his back, enabling them to kick him again where it hurt most, amid shrieks of laughter.

It was more than Dodd could stand. He pushed forward like the chivalrous hero of some boys' book of adventure, and cleared the brutes away from the prostrate man.

44

'Prisoner,' he said, and then, in the instinctive belief that they would understand him better if he shouted and if he spoke ungrammatically he continued in a louder tone, pointing to the captive. 'Prisoner. He prisoner. He not to be hurt.'

Looking round at the lowering expressions of the Portuguese, he realized that they still did not understand, and he tried to make use of what he knew of Spanish and Portuguese grammatical constructions.

'*Prisonerado*,' he said. '*Captivado, Não damagado.*'

The leader nodded. Clearly he had heard somewhere or other of some silly convention that prisoners were not to be tortured. He broke into rapid speech. Two of his men under his instructions hoisted the dragoon to his feet so that he stood swaying between them. And then, under his further instructions, before Dodd could interfere, three more of his men lowered their pikes and thrust them into his body. The Frenchman, mercifully, was not long dying then, while Dodd looked on horrified and the others grinned at each other. When he was dead they tore his bloodstained clothes from his corpse; one man put on the blue tunic with the red shoulder-knots, while another pulled on the white breeches. Stained as they were, they were better garments than those discarded in their favour. Then they made ready to move on. The leader tapped

Dodd on the shoulder and by his gestures clearly indicated that they expected him to accompany them.

'*Inglezes*?' demanded Dodd, pointing.

The leader shook his head and pointed in nearly the opposite direction, and once more insisted in pantomime on his accompanying them. His verbal explanation included the word '*Franceses*'; obviously he was trying to tell Dodd what he knew already, that the whole French army lay between him and the English. Dodd pointed to himself and then south-eastwards.

'*Tejo*,' he said. '*Alhandra. Lisboa.*'

The leaded nodded and shrugged. He had heard vaguely of the Tagus and of Lisbon, but the river was full fifty miles away and the city a hundred; he had no real belief in their existence. He sloped his musket and signed to Dodd to come with them. The southerly route they seemed determined upon was not far out of his way, so that he joined them in their march without misgiving.

Two months of guerilla warfare had already taught the Portuguese some elements of military methods. At orders from the leader one man went far to the right, another to the left, a third ahead. With flank guards and advance guard in this fashion there was small chance of their meeting the enemy unexpectedly. They dropped down the steep slope, and turned their faces up the path. The dead horse lay there, already stripped of everything worth carrying away. Farther back lay the dead Portuguese. Someone waved his hand towards the body and made some remark about João. Everybody laughed a little—laughed at the memory of the dead João who did not have the sense to take to the rocks when pursued by a horseman. That was all the epitaph João received.

Dodd never discovered, to his dying day, what had been going on just before his arrival on the scene of the skirmish—who had been fighting, and in what numbers. He could only guess that some reconnoitring or foraging party of dragoons had collided with some detachment of the irregulars.

How the men he was now accompanying came to be in their strategical position overlooking the gorge when clearly there had been hand-to-hand fighting higher up he could not conceive, nor what had happened to the rest of the combatants, nor why his friends displayed no anxiety to rejoin their main body. Portuguese irregulars were not distinguished for the discipline which prevailed, for example, in the Ninety-Fifth Foot.

They knew their way about the country. They quitted the good track upon which the march had begun in favour of one much less obvious and practicable, and tramped along without hesitation, up hills and down them, over fords and through forests, the while the

47

sun sank lower and lower. Then they turned into a path which led straight up into the highest hills. It wound round the edge of some precipices and went straight up the face of others, becoming indistinguishable from a dry watercourse in the process. Even the marching powers of a man of the Ninety-Fifth were strained to the utmost. Dodd had fed badly for two days now, and he had marched much. His head began to swim and his heart to beat distressfully against his ribs as he toiled along behind the big Portuguese leader. He began to slip and fall at the difficult parts, borne down by the weight of his weapons and pack. When he fell the man behind trod on his feet while the man in front made no attempt to wait for him. Darkness fell, and still they struggled along the stony way, while Dodd felt as though he must soon sink under his fatigue.

What roused him at the end of that nightmare climb was a harsh challenge from the slopes above, which was instantly answered by his party. The pace slackened; they stumbled over a few yards more of rocky path, and round a corner where Dodd had the impression of a vertical drop hundreds of feet high on his right hand. Here there was a clear space—a wide shelf on the mountain side, apparently, where a score of bivouac fires were burning, with the little groups seated round them.

The leader tapped Dodd's shoulder and led

him forward through the lines of fires to the farthest end of the shelf. Here a corner of the rock made some sort of shallow cave, at the mouth of which a big fire was burning, and where two lanterns on poles shed additional light. Seated by the fire were two priests in their black clothes, and between them a burly man in a shabby blue uniform with faded silver lace at collar and wrists. Dodd's guides approached and made some sort of salute and, as far as Dodd could understand, accounted for Dodd's presence.

'*Capitão Mor*,' he continued explanatorily to Dodd, and then left him.

A *Capitão Mor*—Great Captain—as Dodd vaguely understood, was a great man in Portugal, something midway between a squire and a Lord-Lieutenant, ex-officio commander of the feudal levies of the district. This one looked Dodd up and down and said something to him in Portuguese.

'*Não comprehend*,' said Dodd.

The *Capitão Mor* tried again, speaking with difficulty in what Dodd guessed must be another language—French, presumably.

'*Não comprehend*,' said Dodd.

The *Capitão Mor* turned to one of the priests at his side, who in turn addressed him in some other language, concluding with the sign of the cross and the gesture of counting his rosary. Dodd guessed what that meant, and hotly denied the imputation.

'*Não, não, não,*' he said. There were Roman Catholics in his regiment, good enough fellows too, but Dodd's early upbringing had laid so much stress on the wickedness of Popery that even now he felt insulted at being asked if he was a Roman Catholic. He would not put up with being questioned by Papists and Portuguese any longer. He pointed to himself and then out into the night.

'*Tejo,*' he said. '*Lisboa.* Me. Tomorrow.'

The others made no sign of comprehension.

'*Tejo,*' he repeated angrily, pounding on his chest. 'Lisbon. *Tejo, Tejo, Tejo.*'

The three conferred together.

'*Tejo?*' said the *Capitão Mor* to Dodd interrogatively.

'*Sim. Tejo, Tejo, Tejo.*'

'Bernardino,' said the *Capitão Mor*, turning to one of the other groups at the fires.

Someone came over to them. He was in the usual rags, but on his head was an English infantry shako—the regimental figures '43' shone in the firelight. He was only a boy, and he grinned at Dodd in friendly fashion while the *Capitão Mor* gave his orders. Dodd heard the words '*Tejo*' and '*Lisboa*'—blessed words. Bernadino nodded and grinned again. Then the *Capitão Mor* turned to Dodd again with words and gesture of polite dismissal, and Bernadino led him away to another fireside.

Over this fire hung an iron pot from which came a smell of onions which to Dodd's famished interior was utterly heavenly. Bernardino politely made him sit down, found a wooden dish from somewhere, and ladled into it a generous portion of stew from the pot. He brought him a hunk of bread, and, still grinning, invited him to eat—an invitation Dodd did not need to have repeated. He pulled his knife and spoon from his pack and ate like a wolf. Yet even at that moment, dizzy with fatigue, the ruling passion asserted itself.

'*Lisboa*? *Tejo*?' he asked of Bernadino.

'*Sim. Sim.*' Bernadino nodded and said a good deal more, until, realizing that he was quite unintelligible, he fell back on pantomime. It takes much complicated gesture to convey the abstract of 'tomorrow', but he succeeded at last, and Dodd was satisfied. When he had finished his meal his head began to nod on to his breast. He coiled himself up in his greatcoat and fell asleep, revelling in the delicious warmth of the fire. But he mistrusted the military efficiency of the Portuguese. He took off neither his equipment nor his boots, and he slept with his rifle within reach.

CHAPTER SEVEN

During the three days' march that followed Bernardino was almost convinced that this big Englishman whom he had been deputed to

51

guide was slightly mad. He had only one thought—it might be said he had only one word. What he wanted was to reach the Tagus. Nothing else would satisfy him. He would not rest a moment more than necessary; he was always up at the first streak of dawn; he insisted on striding along even when Bernardino was whimpering with fatigue. Bernardino had not heard of the Indian pilgrims whose one wish it was to bathe in the Ganges, but once or twice he had encountered Spaniards or Portuguese who were set on visiting some particular shrine—Santiago di Compostella or some other—and who also were slightly mad, and he came to class Dodd with them in his mind. He explained to everyone they met that he had a mad Englishman in his charge whose one wish in life was to set eyes on the Tagus; in Bernardino's opinion this was just as remarkable as that the long rifle the Englishman carried would (so he had been assured) kill a man with deadly accuracy at half a mile. Bernadino's ambition was, after having gratified the Englishman's strange passion for the Tagus, to lure him into sight of a Frenchman and then see the feat performed.

There were plenty of people for Bernardino to tell all this to, because the country through which they were passing was not laid waste. The proclamations commanding this to be done had been issued—every priest and every alcalde had one—but the country was not in the direct line of march of the contending armies and Wellington had not been able to come there in person and see his orders carried out. It would take more than a mere proclamation to make a wretched peasant burn his crops and his farm and send his womenfolk to Lisbon while he himself went up into the hills to starve. Here and there were patches of mined country where some *Capitão Mor* of unusual energy had swept the district with his militia, but elsewhere there were flocks of sheep and herds of cattle, and fields under the plough making ready for the winter sowing.

Dodd shook his head at sight of all this; if the French army should come this way they would be able to demonstrate their practice that every village should be able to feed a battalion for a week or a division for a day. He was surly towards the village people on whom Bernardino billeted him each night. He could not even accept the pleasant advances of the women in his billets; the women ran delighted eyes over his burly inches, and would have liked to tell him how much they missed their husbands whom the conscription had swept away, but Dodd turned away from them angrily. Their refusal to destroy all their possessions was imperilling his regiment.

There came a day when the road along which they were marching climbed up a small slope, and then descended into a green valley.

At the crest Bernardino stopped and pointed forwards dramatically.

'*Eis*!' he said. '*Tejo.*'

He gazed at Dodd expectantly to see what effect this long wished for spectacle would have upon him, and he was woefully disappointed. For Dodd merely gazed for a moment across the flat land to where the vast green river ran turbulently in its rocky bed, and then strode on carelessly. And when the country track they were following joined the main high road above the river's bank he turned along it to the right without stopping for Bernardino's guidance and without another glance at the river he had been asking for for at least the last three days, the river he had walked sixty-five miles to see. Bernardino pulled him by the sleeve to call his attention to it again, but Dodd merely shook him off.

'*Lisboa,*' said Dodd, pointing forwards remorselessly.

Bernardino could only resign himself to another sixty-five mile march to Lisbon.

Only for brief stretches does the Tagus run through fertile, cultivated land. Before very long their march took them once again into a stony, sandy desert, a high plateau towering far above the water's edge, and cut up here and there by ravines, at the bottom of which torrential watercourses boiled over their rocky beds on their way to join the main river. The great high road passed across this plateau as straight as a bullet, leaping each ravine in turn by a high stone bridge; at rare intervals a little village lay beside the road whose inhabitants gained a scanty living by keeping flocks of stunted sheep on the scanty herbage of the hills.

Dodd had twice marched along this road with his regiment; he remembered its main features, and as each remembered characteristic came into view he grew more fevered in his expectancy, and pressed forward until Bernardino was nearly running to keep pace with him. The morning came when Alhandra, the town where the Lines came down to the river, was only thirty miles away— one long march. Inside the Lines was the British army, the regiment, everything that Dodd held dear.

Then they met a group of Portuguese irregulars beside the road, at a point where the river left it to make a great loop round the end of a mountain spur. They were not quite as irregular as some Portuguese Dodd had seen; some had genuine fragments of uniform, some of them had muskets, and some of them had bayonets and military cross-belts. They stopped Dodd and Bernardino, and the leader addressed them with harsh questions. Bernardino answered with the loquacity and self-importance natural to him—a long explanation of the Englishman whose one wish was to see Lisbon again, whose rifle would kill a man at a mile, the orders given them by the *Capitão Mor* and much more besides.

The man addressed laughed harshly at all this, shaking his head. He told Bernardino that the French barred the way to Alhandra and Lisbon, and Bernardino looked blankly at Dodd. But Dodd understood nothing of what was said, and strongly disapproved of all this waste of time over idle gossip. He made to push through the group.

'*Lisboa*,' said Dodd. '*Alhandra*.'

They held him back, explaining to him in voluble Portuguese. He caught their drift at last; he heard the word '*Franceses*'.

'*Franceses*?' he asked.

'*Sim, sim, Franceses*,' they answered, pointing down the road.

And at that moment, as if to accentuate their words, the sentry a quarter of a mile down the road uttered a loud shout, and came running towards them, gesticulating. Everyone looked to see to what he was calling their attention; they climbed on the stone wall bordering the road, and gazed along it. A long column of horsemen was trotting towards them; it only took one glance to recognize French dragoons.

At once everyone was seized with the confusion of the undisciplined. Some made to run away, some towards the dragoons. Some even pointed their muskets towards the French, who were ten times as far away as a

56

bullet could reach. Dodd alone produced a practicable plan—he had fought in so many skirmishes by now that his reactions were instinctive. He glanced back at the last bridge—but he decided that he could not rely on these feeble soldiers to hold a bridge against a charge of dragoons. To the right the ground sloped away smoothly, and save for a few stone walls offered no protection against horsemen. Only to the left was there safety— the ground rose steeply only one field away, and was rocky and broken.

'This way!' shouted Dodd. 'Come this way, you fools!'

The universal language of gesture and example explained what he wanted. Everybody bundled over the stone wall and across the field and up into the rocks. Somebody's musket which had been carried at full cock went off without hurting anyone. Once they had started running they would have gone on until they dropped, doubtless, but Dodd yelled himself hoarse, dropped behind a convenient rock, and the others at length imitated his example. Bernardino, squeaking with excitement, was kneeling beside Dodd and peering over the rock.

'*Tirar!*' he was saying, or some such word.

What he meant was obvious from the way he pointed to Dodd's rifle and then at the French. But Dodd shook his head; the range was far too long. Bernardino wailed his

57

disappointment.

The colonel commanding the dragoons down in the road had no thought of attacking the light-footed men among the rocks. He had had too many lessons in guerilla warfare by now—he had led his men the length and breadth of Portugal and Spain in incessant contact with pests like these. All he wanted to do was to take his regiment along the road in peace and find out whether there were formed troops along it; the presence of irregulars could be taken for granted. What had to be done was to keep the enemy from the roadside so that they could not take long shots into the vulnerable column. At his orders a troop of dragoons trotted into the field, dismounted on the far side, and while some stayed holding the horses the remainder took their short carbines and scattered among the rocks, while the rest of the long column of horsemen filed along the road. Dodd gazed down at the scattered dragoons. In their long boots and hampered by their helmets and their trailing sabres they were the most unwieldy skirmishers imaginable. He had no fear of them, and it would be tempting to evade them and harass the long column behind them. He looked round at his motley companions; they were looking to him for a lead. With a yell he sprang to his feet, waving his arms to his men, and ran, not towards the road, but parallel to it, along the steep side of the hill. The others hesitated, but Bernardino seemed to have grasped Dodd's plan, and when he called to them explanatorily they followed. The covering dragoons fired at them ineffectually with their carbines; not a shot told, and Dodd, with the others yelling behind him, ran panting over the rocks diagonally down to the road again where the dragoons were riding three by three. He fired into the thick of them, and a man fell from his saddle. Instantly the others fired too; it seemed as if one or two of the bullets miraculously hit their marks. There was con-fusion in the road. Some young officer who still had not learnt his lesson drew his sword and set his horse at the rocks calling to the others to follow him.

Horses fell with a crash among the stones, and Dodd, reloading with the speed of years of drill, shot the officer whose horse alone kept his feet. Other dragoons fired wildly from the saddle; a few dismounted and began a more careful fire from the side of the road. It was only then that the covering flank guard began to come into action again. The clumsily equipped men had had to labour across the field and over the walls along to where the irregulars had preceded them. Dodd saw them coming and yelled again to his men. Bernardino, mad with excitement, abetted him shrilly. Next moment they were all running diagonally up the hill again, leaving their clumsy pursuers far behind. They made their breathless way again along the spur to head off the column once more, and then again they rushed down the slope to fire at the helpless horsemen.

There was no pity in Dodd's mind; it was his business to kill Frenchmen, and if the Frenchmen were not in a position to try to kill him in return so much the better. He fired pitilessly into the long column, reloaded and fired again, and his companions did the same when they came up. The flanking party came up belatedly to drive them off, but for yet a third time they were able to get along the spur and repeat their manoeuvre. The maddened dragoons down in the road could do nothing. It had been their fate to be sniped at thus over a thousand miles of road—small wonder that they burnt in their exasperation the villages through which they passed, and hanged anyone unfortunate enough to fall into their hands.

Today relief came to them where the mountain spur ended and the road came down close to the river bank. Dodd eyed the narrowing triangle between road and river and called his men off. He would not risk being hemmed in there, and he was wearied with much running among the rocks. He shouted, and he gesticulated, and then he walked back up the spur. Below him the cavalry trotted on down the road. The last man in the long column turned in his saddle and shook his fist and shouted his exasperation, at which everyone with Dodd laughed hysterically.

It was an exhilarating introduction to war for the Tagus-side militia. There were half a dozen dead men and half a dozen dead horses along the road, to be stripped of their clothes and accoutrements, and not one of their own party had been hurt. They looked at Dodd respectfully now, and, as for Bernardino, his eyes shone with admiration for the big, burly rifleman in his black-braided green coat. He walked along beside him looking up at him almost with a dog's devotion, and when Dodd sat down on a boulder overlooking the road, with his chin on his hands, Bernardino sat down too, quietly, so as not to disturb the great man's meditations.

There was much for Dodd to think about. This, the last road towards Lisbon, was blocked with French troops, apparently. He was cut off from his countrymen and his regiment. He had failed in his endeavour to march round the French army. The latter seemed to have swerved to its left and then recoiled, which made it appear most likely that they had reached the Lines. The one hope left was that they might be in retreat—the cavalry were certainly on the road towards France, but the movement of a single regiment of cavalry was by no means indicative of the movement of a whole army. Far more probably they were only looking for means of crossing the Tagus.

All that Dodd could decide was that he must find a secure shelter until he could discover enough about the French movements to make fresh plans now that his first plan was upset.

Dodd was not exasperated or cast down at the new development. The soldier with years of campaigning behind him has, perforce, acquired a philosophic outlook towards turns of fortune. If one plan goes wrong there is need to make another, that is all. And, as for despair—there was no room for despair in Dodd's make-up. The regiment had taught him that he must do his duty or die in the attempt; a simple enough religion fit for his simple mind. As long as there was breath in his body or a thought in his mind he must struggle on; as long as he went on trying there was no need to meditate on success or failure. The only reward for the doing of his duty would be the knowledge that his duty was being done. That was how honour called; and glory—the man in the ranks did not bother with glory, nor did the men a century later who died in the poison gas at Ypres.

The Portuguese round Dodd were chattering like a nest of magpies, telling each other over and over again of their individual exploits in the recent skirmish, and every time with embellishments and additions. They displayed their trophies to each other, they romped and they gambolled. They were not like the hardbitten militia of the Beira whom

Dodd had encountered earlier, who had fought in three invasions of Portugal, who had seen their homes destroyed and their women ravished; this was the first time the tide of war had reached these out-of-the-way banks of the Tagus.

Dodd wondered grimly what these men would do in action against a French light infantry regiment, and realized that he would probably see it happen soon enough. He must make preparations against the arrival of the French Army. First, he must discover their village, their headquarters. He searched in his mind for words of Portuguese. He poked the leader in the ribs and tried the word for 'town'.

'*Vilha?*' he asked.

The other seemed dazed at the question. Truth to tell, there was no town within thirty miles. Dodd thought again, and inspiration came to him.

'*Posada?*' he asked. Where the wine shop was, there would be the village.

A great light dawned upon the faces of the listening Portuguese. Of course there was immediate need to visit the *posada*. They could not understand how they had come to forget the possibility of celebrating the recent glorious victory. Everyone shouted at once. Everyone caught up his bundle of booty and began to bustle about in preparation for a triumphant return home. With beckonings of welcome they led Dodd down the road, a mile or so along it, and up a narrow, rocky lane over the spur of the hill. There, nestling in a little valley surrounded by towering rocks, lay their little village, twenty stone houses in all. The houses were grouped with no method about a central open space; there were huge stinking heaps of manure here and there; a little rivulet rushing through the village down to the Tagus served at once as a source of drinking water and as a sewer. The women and old men and children turned out to witness their triumphant entry. Lean chickens scrambled about the stones; four long strips of hand-picked land stretching down towards the green river showed where the villagers wrung their wretched living from the ungrateful soil. There were pigs to be seen, and up the sides of the valley were tethered cows just managing to keep alive among the few blades of grass among the rocks.

The ragged women and the nearly naked children—no child wore more than one garment—stood wondering as they marched in, waving their weapons and their trophies.

The men gathered outside the wine shop, escorting Dodd with ceremony to a seat on the stone benches.

Wine made its appearance at once, in wooden cups. Everyone was drinking, talking, shouting. Everyone eyed Dodd as they pointed him out as the marvellous Englishman who had beaten the French with the necessary assistance of the valiant villagers. As an afterthought Dodd's cup, half empty, was taken from him, and a new one .brought him, full of the best wine the *posada* boasted—*vinho valeroso*, as he was assured on every side.

When Dodd made the gesture of eating they brought him food, and everyone else, like children, decided they must eat too. The men squatted here and there round the *posada* while the women brought food, but eating did not interfere in the least with conversation nor—most decidedly not—with drinking. The situation had every appearance of developing into a wild village spree, one of those few marvellous days when the frugal Portuguese peasant could forget the cost of anything, forget the need to work, forget the precariousness of existence. Bernardino, who naturally had the morals of a muleteer, seeing that was his profession, was caressing a girl in a secluded corner. Already someone had produced a guitar, and some were singing and some were dancing, when Dodd heaved himself to his feet. All eyes turned upon him while he picked out three of the young men and beckoned them to follow him. He led them out of the village up the stony lane again. Two of them he stationed within sight of the high road. He handled their muskets; he pointed up and down the road, peering out under his hand; he seemed to catch sight of something on the road, pointed the musket, called out 'bang', held one of the two still, and pushed the other with the gesture of running back to the village. They grasped his meaning, grinning broadly and nodding. Pointing to the sun, and then to the west, he indicated the length of their watch. The third man he sent up the hillside where the view was more extensive.

Then he went back to the village. There was no position that he could see where twenty peasants could defy the attack of a hundred thousand men, although there was comfort to be found in the sight of the precipitous, rocky heights on each side of the ravine. He walked down to the river bank. The turbulent green water was pouring down over its rocky shelves, the whole surface marked with ripples and eddies. So wide was it that details on the farther bank were hardly to be made out.

Then, far down the river, something appeared round the bend which made him catch his breath with excitement. It was a white boat; as he looked he saw the flash of oars. He picked his way along the stony water's edge towards it. It was fighting its way upstream, taking advantage of the eddies inside the curve. There was something unusual about the deliberation of the strokes of the oars; Dodd recognized the rhythm at once—he had been landed from so many transports that he could not help but know the Navy stroke. The boat drew nearer and nearer. Dodd could see the gun mounted in the bow and the flutter of the white ensign at the stern. He could see the officer at the tiller and the men bending over their oars. He rushed along the bank, waving and shouting, but the boat pulled steadily on. In the long pull up from Alhandra so many Portuguese had waved to them from the bank that the crew did not give him a second thought. If only he had been wearing a red coat!

The boat rounded the curve and the officer stood up in the stern sheets to look up the next reach. Satisfied that no French were trying to cross the river he sat down again and pulled the tiller over. The boat swung round and edged into mid-stream to catch the full force of the current; its patrol was over. The current whirled it back round the curve at four times the speed at which it had ascended. Dodd still ran and waved and shouted, to no avail. The officer found time to wave a friendly arm to him, and a few minutes later the boat had vanished round the curve, beneath the beetling cliffs. There was nothing that Dodd could do save to plod back to the village and resume his plans for the discomfiture of the French in this quarter.

CHAPTER EIGHT

'Precipices! My God, nothing but precipices!' said Sergeant Godinot, staring up at the lines of Torres Vedras. 'And there is a fortress as strong as Rodrigo on the top of that hill—look at the guns in the embrasures. We shall have some fighting to do before we reach Lisbon after all, you men. Three miles of precipices so far.'

'You didn't tell us about this at the depot, sergeant,' said Fournier, where he stood beside him.

'The English had not seen fit to inform me of it,' said Godinot, and added, under his breath, 'Nor anyone else either.'

'What in the name of God is that in that ravine?' asked Dubois, pointing.

Everyone looked, but no one offered an explanation. All they could see was that a whole valley penetrating the Lines had been stuffed up with something or other. At that distance it was impossible to see, and from their experience it was impossible to realize that a hundred thousand olive trees, roots, branches and all, had been flung into the ravine to make an entanglement that not even a mouse, let alone a man, could penetrate.

'More precipices,' said Godinot, as the march of the company opened up a view of a new sector. Another long strip of a bare hillside had been dug or blasted away, leaving a ten-foot scarp that a man could only mount with a ladder; and redoubts at each end of the scarp, with guns mounted to enfilade it, indicated what would be the fate of anyone who attempted to do so.

'Red-coats up there,' said Godron, pointing. The British army was in position behind the Lines to support the hordes of militia who manned the redoubts.

Still the company marched on. The French advance guard was feeling to its left in an endeavour to find if there was any end to this line of fortifications against which it had stumbled. Sergeant Godinot and his friends were in the extreme flank company, marching continually southwards parallel to the Lines. On their right a bare valley, three-quarters of a mile wide, extended to the foot of the entrenchments, and this valley had been swept clean as if with a broom. Not a tree, not a bush, not a fragment of rock had been allowed to remain. Troops forming up for an assault would do so under heavy fire and without a vestige of cover.

'Somebody's worked damned hard,' growled Fournier.

'Not as hard as you'll have to work soon, old boy, when we break through,' laughed Godinot, expressing an opinion he did not feel in the least.

'Break through? Do you think we're going to break through *that*? Never in your life,' said Fournier. He had only been a soldier for a year, but he knew the militarily impossible when he saw it.

'Well, we'll find a way round,' said Godinot optimistically.

A puff of smoke shot from a redoubt, and a cannon-ball screamed over their heads and plumped into the hillside above them.

'We are trespassing on Their Excellencies' territory,' said Godinot.

The captain at the head of the company took the hint, and led the little column diagonally up the hill a trifle before marching on.

There were frequent stumbles and oaths in the ranks, for there was only the rough countryside to march upon. There was no road, or track even, here outside the Lines. Before long every man in the ranks was cursing and complaining as he staggered along over the uneven ground, bowed under his pack, until at last there was no breath left even for curses, and the only sounds to be heard were the clash of nailed boots on rock and the creaking of accoutrements. Once or twice there was a welcome halt, but each time the colonel rode up and the company had to move on again. As much information as was possible must be gained in the shortest possible time regarding this amazing phenomenon, and

70

these stony hills were no place for cavalry. Up hills they went, so steep that progress had to be made on hands and knees, and down valleys. The intervals between companies was growing longer and longer, as Sergeant Godinot saw when he looked back; the advance guard was growing desperately thin. Still they marched, until at the last crest they saw ahead of them what must be a river valley—the Tagus at last.

'Did you say we were going to find a way round, sergeant?' asked Fournier with a sneer, pointing to their right front.

In that direction there was a gleam of water, a hint of marsh and of flooded fields, stretching clear down to where two more huge redoubts towered above the Tagus bank. A tributary of the Tagus had been dammed at its mouth to make a morass four miles long to fill the gap between the fortifications in the hills and the Tagus. Even Godinot, conscientiously anxious to keep his section cheerful, had no reply to make to that. He could only look wordlessly, and he continued to look when the order to halt was given and the exhausted men sank to the ground. Three staff officers who had accompanied them on foot, their bridles over their arms, gazed down at the river with their telescopes. Then they turned back, wordlessly.

Godinot guessed what sort of message they would have to take back to headquarters—

71

they displayed their disappointment and dismay in every gesture—still he did his best to be cheerful.

'They'll have found something better than this out on the right,' he said.

But his tentative optimism was received with a chilling silence. Even men stupid with fatigue and hunger had more sense than to imagine that an enemy who had so carefully fortified this end would leave the other end unguarded.

That, of course, was an eminently correct deduction. This outer line (there were inner ones too) extended for twenty-two miles across the base of the triangle enclosed between the sea and the Tagus, so that in the top of the triangle, in Lisbon and the surrounding country, the British army and the Portuguese population could find secure shelter while the enemy starved outside. British ingenuity and Portuguese hard work could make a position impregnable even in the days before barbed wire and machine-guns.

The captain summoned his four sergeants and issued his orders.

'Sergeant Bossin's section will do picket duty tonight. I will attend to the posting of the sentries myself. The other sections may bivouac and cook.'

The captain tried to meet the eyes of his sergeants when he said this, but his gaze wavered. It was hard to say those words and face the reproach in the faces of the others. There was a chill wind blowing, and a thin rain was beginning to fall.

'Do we bivouac where we are, sir?' asked Godinot. 'Yes. Those are the orders.'

The captain knew that it was a bad disciplinary move to blame the hardship the men had to suffer upon higher authority, but he had to excuse himself.

Back went the sergeants to where the exhausted men lay upon the bleak hillside. So weary were they that the news that there was to be no issue of rations was received without a complaint. The men had ceased, in fact, to expect a ration issue, and, marching as they had been in contact with the enemy, they had had no chance to plunder food.

Wearily they had made their preparations for the night. Half a dozen volunteers—the ones whose feet were least damaged—began to crawl about the hill cutting bushes for fuel. Fournier and Lebrun, who boasted the possession of a blanket which they carried turn and turn about, began to erect it like a tiny tent. Soon half a dozen wretched little fires were alight, giving much smoke and very little heat. Only round one fire was there any bustle of expectation. Here a pot was actually being hung over the flames, and one man was preparing the meat for the evening meal for himself and his intimate friends. It was a little white dog he had seen at the beginning of that day's march, and had instantly shot. For the rest of the day he had carried it slung by the paws from his belt and now, in quite a matter-of-fact way, he proceeded to skin it and disembowel it and joint it, throwing the meat piece by piece into the pot. Other men looked on hungrily, but it was only a little dog, and they could not expect a share.

Someone carried a platter of the stew to the captain in his solitary bivouac, but although he looked at it with longing, and sniffed at its heavenly savour, he refused it sadly, and turned again to gnawing at his flinty bread. He could not eat meat unless all his men had at least a taste of it.

Darkness fell, and the fires began to die away. The wretched men huddled their cloaks closer about their ragged bodies, and tried to burrow into the earth in an effort to shelter themselves from the penetrating cold. They were only boys, these men of the Eighth Corps, new recruits bundled together into hastily formed battalions and sent out on the long and dreary road to Portugal, untrained, unseasoned, ill-equipped. The man who sent them was at that time progressing about his provinces displaying to a dazzled people the marvellous new wife he had won by right of conquest—a real Hapsburg princess, daughter of fifty emperors.

The wind blew colder with the falling of the night. The men muttered and groaned as they turned backwards and forwards seeking some sort of warmth or comfort. Yet their rest was not broken when the sentries challenged, for that was a cry to which they were accustomed. For the captain went the round three times that night, to see that the sentries were alert and at their posts. Vigilance was necessary, for Portuguese had been known to creep into the ranks of sleeping men and cut half a dozen throats before crawling away again undetected.

CHAPTER NINE

Even the young soldiers of the Eighth Corps could look at a river and guess by the direction of its flow whether they were in advance or retreat.

'What's this, sergeant?' asked young Bernhard. 'Are we going home?'

For the regiment was at the head of a long column marching up the high road along the Tagus bank away from the Lines.

'Perhaps God knows, but I don't,' said Godinot.

'Perhaps we're going to find Godinot's uncle,' said Fournier.

'Let us hope so,' said Godinot. He himself could not hope so; he could not imagine that they were about to pass by the bridgeless

75

Tagus and join with the distant Army of the South.

'No,' said Fournier, 'Bernhard is right. We're going home. Back to decent billets. And all of us are to be given a new pair of shoes and let us hope Godron will get another pair of breeches before the Spanish ladies lay eyes on him and swoon in ecstasy.'

There was a laugh at that. The boys could actually laugh, now that a definite move had been made and they were marching in a new direction.

They passed a dead horse at the side of the road.

'The dragoons are in front of us, then,' said Godinot, looking at the thing, which was just beginning to swell with corruption.

'Why should it be one of ours?' asked Godron. There was no fraction of its equipment left on it.

'By the brand on its flank, son,' replied Godinot. 'When are you going to learn your trade?'

'But if it's one of ours,' said Bernhard thoughtfully, 'and the dragoons are in front, it looks like a retreat, doesn't it?'

'Maybe,' said Godinot, and then he hardened his heart, for he did not want these boys' hopes raised too high. 'But they'd be sent back out of the way whatever we were going to do—attack the lines or stand still. I expect we're only sent this way to act as flank guard to

76

look after the river.'

That cast them down: the prospect of lingering further in Portugal was abhorrent to them. There was no further conversation until another incident occurred to stimulate it afresh.

A staff officer came clattering up the paved road along the column to where the colonel rode at the head.

'Orders,' said Bernhard sagely. 'And orders always mean trouble.'

He was right. Somewhere farther back the road had diverged from the river in order to cross at a more convenient point a double-headed spur of hills which ran at right angles down to the river. Up into the mass of tangled country lying between road and river diverged a narrow, stony lane. Here the battalion halted for a moment, and the rumour—as always, no one knew who was responsible for it—ran down the ranks that billets lay at the end of the lane. But the colonel clearly did not expect a hospitable reception at the billets, seeing that he pushed the battalion up the lane in advance-guard formation.

'This looks like the end of our retreat,' said Godron.

'But billets tonight, boys,' said Fournier. 'And soup for supper.'

At that very moment a shot rang out at the head of the column, followed by half a dozen more. The column halted, went on, halted again, while the firing increased and died away and revived. Godinot's friends at the rear of the column did not bother to crane their necks to see what was happening in front. This sort of skirmish occurred two or three times a day to a column marching in Portugal. Then the captain came back down the column, his drummer behind him. He scaled the steep side of the lane and stood looking up the hills for a space before he turned and beckoned to his waiting company. They climbed the bank with stoical nonchalance.

'Chase those fellows over into the river,' said the captain.

Everyone knew what he had to do. The company spread out in a long thin line and pushed slowly up the steep hill. Right at the summit occasional shots and puffs of smoke indicated where the advance guard was in action. For some distance they met with no opposition, but half-way up the hill a puff of smoke jetted out from behind a rock and a bullet crackled overhead.

The man who fired it sprang up and dashed ahead of them up the hill. The line of skirmishers bulged for a minute as some of the hotheads made as though to run after him, and then settled down again to a steady advance. Higher up there were more men in ambush, more shots fired. Someone in the skirmishing line fell with a crash and a clatter. Here and there men fired back.

'Wait until you are sure,' shouted Godinot to his section.

Some of them looked round at him and grinned. In the friendly relations which existed between non-commissioned officers and men in the French army they had often had arguments with him regarding marksmanship.

They were nearing the top of the hill. Whoever was opposing them there would find his retreat cut off if he was not careful.

'There's an Englishman there!' suddenly shouted Fournier. 'A green Englishman!'

They all caught sight of him; he was calling and gesticulating to the men gathered at the summit. Everyone recognized his uniform, and, further, everyone realized the purport of his gesticulations. The captain, waving his sword, rushed to the front and called to his men to follow him in a final dash, but the green-coated soldier had timed his stand to a nicety. He and his band turned and ran helter-skelter along the summit, neatly avoiding being driven down into the river.

Without orders, the French inclined to their right and ran to head them off, while the advance guard with whom the Portuguese had originally been engaged followed in hot pursuit. One of the Portuguese missed his footing and fell rolling down the slope, and before he could regain his feet Godinot's bayonet was through him. Fournier at Godinot's side, wild with excitement, stabbed

79

him too, and the man died writhing with rage and pain.

The skirmish lost all trace of order up here on the wild mountain top. When a skirmishing line begins to run in broken country and with frequent changes of direction it soon ceases to be a line. The two French companies broke into little groups ranging hither and thither over the hillside, while the sky grew dark and torrents of rain poured down to add to the confusion. In that nightmare country of tall rocks and scrubby trees and low bushes the battle was fought out to an indecisive end. The timorous and the weary among the French found ample opportunity of withdrawing from the struggle, and crouching for shelter and concealment in clefts in the rocks, while the brave and the headstrong lost their way. Yet there were still musket shots spitting out here and there in the gathering gloom. Men were still meeting their deaths in the disordered battle.

Godinot, pushing up a little ravine with two or three followers, met Lebrun and Fournier coming down it, and between them they were half leading, half carrying someone else—Godron.

'The Englishman shot him,' explained Fournier.

'The Englishman?'

'Yes, by God!'

'Where's he wounded?'

'In the stomach.'

There was a pause at that. Everyone knew what a stomach wound involved, and everyone knew—it had been enjoined upon them so often—that only the cowards withdrew from a fight to help the wounded home. Yet everyone knew, too, that they could not leave a wounded man—not even a dying man—where Portuguese irregulars might reach him.

Godinot was saved from the dilemma by a long roll of a drum far behind him. Then the drum beat to a new rhythm, a long roll and three beats followed by a short roll and three beats, repeated. It was the retreat. A greatcoat with two muskets thrust through the sleeves and pocket slits made some sort of stretcher for Godron, and between them they carried him back to where the two companies were re-assembling on the crest above the lane. The sun had set now, but the clouds had parted in the west, and permitted a little watery, dying light. The captain was a sad man as the sergeants made their reports. So-and-so was missing and someone else. And someone else was dead—they had seen him fall, and brought back his things from his pack. The captain looked darkly up the hill, and over to the fading west. This was a defeat, and he could not avenge it as yet. He could not think of plunging his weary men into that tangle of rocks in darkness. He could not even think of trying to find the missing men. He hoped that

81

they were dead rather than in Portuguese hands. He kept the company waiting while darkness fell, to be rewarded by the return of one or two of the missing, and then, reluctantly, he led the company down the hill and down the lane to where a cluster of stone cottages marked the billets of the battalion.

*   *   *

That evening, while little Godron was dying under the surgeon's hands, there was rejoicing in the battalion. Not merely did everyone have a roof over his head—were it only the roof of a filthy cowshed—but everyone had enough to eat. There was a field of potatoes between the village and the river, and although, apparently, efforts had been made to dig them up and throw them into the Tagus there were still great quantities to be found for the digging. And as they had marched in, a nannygoat with two kids had also entered the village, bleating pathetically. That meant soup for everyone, and more than a taste of meat; and not only that, but someone had grabbed a stray, lone chicken running round the dunghills which would be a welcome addition to the officers' mess. There was fuel too—fences and palings in such quantity that there was no need to cut down the fruit trees. Everyone could sit near a great, roaring fire and get warm for the first evening in weeks.

It was sad about the wine. Someone had smashed in all the casks of wine in the cellar of the inn; wine was running everywhere, but for all that there was still enough in the casks for the officers and enough could be scooped off the floor for the men to make them all thoroughly happy. It was a perfectly splendid, riotous evening.

No one gave a second thought to the fact that the goats and the chicken were the only living creatures to be found in the village: they were used to that. Of course it would have added to their enjoyment if a woman or two had been kind enough to remain to help in their entertainment. But that was not important at present; the men had marched too fast and too far lately to have many thoughts to devote to that subject. They were all very happy eating and drinking and revelling in the warmth.

Fournier came and sat down heavily beside Sergeant Godinot.

'Godron's going to die, I suppose?' he began.

'I'm afraid so, poor devil,' said Godinot.

Fournier hesitated a while before he continued:

'Do you remember that day when we were rejoining the battalion after that fatigue we were left behind to do?'

'You mean the day Boyel was killed? Yes.'

'Boyel was Godron's friend.'

'He was my friend too.'

'The same man killed them both,' said Fournier.

'Not likely. How do you know?' asked Godinot.

'It is. I swear it. I saw him as plain as my hand when he killed Boyel. And today—I saw him twice along my musket barrel. How did I come to miss him? How did we all come to miss him the other time? Tell me that.'

'Gently, gently,' said Godinot, noticing the expression on Fournier's face. 'More bullets miss than hit, you know.'

'It will take a lot of bullets to hit that one,' said Fournier.

'Go to sleep and forget about it,' said Godinot. 'You will feel better in the morning.'

Yet it took more than that kindly offhandedness to soothe the superstitious Fournier; it was late when Godinot succeeded.

The fires died down. The battalion slept while the sentries paced their beats round the village. The sentries were on the alert, as well men may be whose lives depend upon it. But no sentry's beat extended down to the river beach, and no one saw a score of dark shadows creep along the water's edge across the mouth of the ravine, leaving the hill of that day's battle for the other one beyond the ravine.

CHAPTER TEN

Next morning the battalion was delighted to hear that they were not to march. Settled here in comfort, with enough to eat and shelter from the weather, they had forgotten their yesterday's yearnings to retreat. But they were not to remain idle, not all of them. Two companies were to stay in their billets to guard the fort and mend their clothes and do whatever else might seem necessary. The other four paraded in light marching order— carrying nothing but their arms and their ammunition—and proceeded to sweep the hill where they had fought yesterday, in search of the brigands who had had the better of them.

It was a careful and highly scientific operation. Three companies were extended until they covered the whole width from road to river, a dozen yards between each man. The four sections of the fourth company were distributed at intervals along the line to supply a solid mass to deal with the brigands when found—the twenty men of a single section could be relied on to do that. Then, with infinite trouble in preserving distance and dressing, they swept across the hill. There were seven miles of it to where the high road came down to the river again, and it took them all day—seven hours of cursing and slipping and stumbling, of dreary waiting in the rain while the line straightened, of beating through dripping wet bushes for hidden enemies, and they found nothing. A few men fired their muskets, but they were only the sort of fools who fire muskets when there is nothing to fire at. There was nobody on the hill at all; the only sign that there had been anyone was the presence of a few naked corpses lying in the rain, one or two of them unknown and therefore Portuguese, the rest the missing Frenchmen of yesterday. Everyone was infuriated, wet, and exhausted when towards evening they stumbled on the pickets of the next battalion down the river and knew that there was no use in searching farther. They marched back through the drenching rain of the bitter night along the high road with its ankle-twisting *pavé*.

It was some consolation when they at last staggered back into the village to find that the headquarters guard had fires ready for them, and hot soup—even though the soup this night had not even a taste of meat and was hardly to be distinguished from plain potatoes and water.

In exasperating three hundred men like this, and wearing out three hundred men's shoe leather, Rifleman Matthew Dodd had done his duty. It had been simple enough, even though it had been tiresome explaining his wishes to the village, not in the least aided by

Bernardino's hopeless misinterpretations of his signs.

The hardest part had been persuading the villagers to destroy what food they could not carry off. They would leave their homes for the hills, they would take their cattle with them, but to destroy food was almost a sacrilege to their frugal minds. Dodd had had to set to work single-handed digging up the potatoes and wheeling them down to the river's brink before they would come to assist him. And he had had to stave in the wine-casks single-handed. Nevertheless, much had been done in the course of the thirty-six hours granted him between the passing of the dragoons and the arrival of the infantry. And when that arrival was at last signalled it had only been elementary strategy to attack them from one hill while the women and the animals had taken refuge in the other; nor was it much more to transfer his men under cover of night to the other hill to evade the most searching attack which Dodd foresaw (he had been a soldier for five years and knew much about the military mind) to be inevitable on the morrow. Simple strategy, but most remarkably effective.

Dodd, that night, sitting by the concealed fire close to the bank of the Tagus, saw no reason at all why he should not continue this harassment for the further two or three days that the French would be in the vicinity before want of food drove them into retreat so that he could emerge and rejoin his beloved regiment.

Two or three days, thought Dodd; the French would have eaten up the supplies by then. Dodd did not estimate correctly what French troops could endure, nor the iron will of the Marshal in command, nor—well as he knew his subject—to quite what lengths of nightmarish, logical absurdity war could be carried. He could not foresee that for three whole months the French were to stay here on the Tagus, starving, while disease and hunger brought down victim after victim, until one man in three had died without setting eyes on an enemy while the English rested and waxed fat in the shelter of the Lines. The ships streaming into Lisbon harbour would bring them English beef and English pork and English bread so that they might rest in comfort until their grim, unseen allies had done their work, until the French army might be sufficiently reduced in numbers to make it possible for them to sally out and engage them on an equality.

It was a strategy as simple as Dodd's, but in both cases it called for iron resolution and contempt for public opinion to carry it out to its fullest, most destructive extent. To compare a simple Rifleman with his Commander-in-Chief may seem sacrilegious, but at least they had been trained in the same school.

The village had worked hard enough in all conscience at saving food from the invaders.

The children had been packed off into the hills with the animals while men and women toiled at emptying the big village barn. Sacks of corn and of maize had been dragged up the steep slopes, women showing themselves as strong as the men at the work. First of all two little side ravines, where arbutus grew thick, had been filled with sacks of corn. When it came to taking the flour, the people had at first appeared to raise objection to Dodd's plans. They talked to each other in loud voices, and turned and explained to Dodd over and over again, but he could not understand. At last big Maria, the mother of the pretty Agostina whom Bernardino favoured, seized Dodd by the arm and dragged him after her, bowed though she was beneath the sack of flour. Over the summit of the hill they went, by a tricky, winding goat track, and down the other side, where the river coursed green and immense at the foot of the slope. A thin track ran down here to the water's edge and ended there abruptly. On each side of the little beach where the path ended the bank of the river rose again in big, beetling cliffs, forty feet high, and the water, running in its winter volume, washed the very foot of them.

Without hesitation Maria hitched up her bulging dress and plunged barelegged into the water, still calling Dodd to follow her. Just below the surface, and responsible for the foaming, frightening eddy here, lay a long ridge of rock. Dodd followed Maria along it, with the water boiling round his knees. Round a corner of the cliff they went, and then before them Dodd could see the ideal sanctuary. It was a little beach in an angle of the cliff, which here had been undercut so that observation even from above would be difficult and most unlikely. There was a small cave, which could be easily enlarged by a few hours' work with a pick. There was no other approach to the beach at all; there was only this underwater ridge—exposed at times of drought, doubtless, which was how the village knew of it—whose existence no one could guess at.

Dodd displayed his enthusiasm for this hiding-place by all the antics of which he was capable, and the village gathered round and revelled in his approval. Hither the old folk were brought, and what few household valuables existed, and as much food as could be carried in the limited time available—the climb was far too long and too steep to permit of everything being done which could be considered necessary. Much of the corn, as has been already mentioned, had to be hidden on the hillside—some even was only poured into a silo near the barn and the mouth of the pit covered with rubbish. The forty-eight hours which opened with the battle with the dragoons and concluded with the battle with the infantry had been busy enough.

Since the last skirmish there had been

peace. Dodd, with Bernardino chuckling delightedly at his side, had lain out on the hill and seen the elaborate attack launched on the other hill—the one they had evacuated. He had counted the force left in the village, and had decided that it was ten times at least too large for him to risk an attack upon it in the absence of the main body. He had seen two graves dug and two men buried in them—one had been little Godron, whom he himself had wounded the night before, although he did not know that. He could easily have lobbed a shot or two at long range among the groups moving among the cottages, but he refrained. There were valuable sheep and cows on the hill behind him, and he did not want to offer any temptation to the French to come up this way and find them.

As they made their way back to the river something on the distant bank caught Dodd's attention—it looked like a long row of glittering beads on an invisible thread. He looked again—the distance was well over half a mile and details were obscure. But his first guess had been correct. The glittering beads were the helmets of a long line of horsemen trotting along the road along the farther bank. It was a long distance to ascertain their nationality. Dodd gazed and gazed, and was still not sure.

'*Portugezes*,' said Bernardino briefly, looking at them under his hand.

91

Bernardino's eyesight was perfectly marvellous—even better than Dodd's—and Dodd was content to take his word for it. He thought he could see high crests to the helmets, and was inclined to agree with him.

So the farther bank was occupied and would be defended against the French should the latter by some miracle find means of crossing the roaring half-mile flood. Dodd nodded his head in solid approval of my Lord of Wellington's arrangement. Could he himself cross over he would find himself among friends who would pass him back to Lisbon and the regiment. But there was no way in which he could cross. There seemed to be no boats at all—that was one matter in which Wellington's order had been obeyed—and Dodd could not swim a stroke. He could only look longingly at the Portuguese dragoons trotting along the opposite bank and turn once more to his present duty of keeping himself out of the hands of the French.

CHAPTER ELEVEN

The Fourth battalion of the Forty-Sixth Infanterie de Ligne had time now to look about itself—for the first time, be it said, since it was formed. Until recently a French infantry regiment had consisted of three battalions, but when the war with Austria was over and the war in Spain was rising to a climax the masses of eighteen-year-old recruits—harvest of two successive anticipated conscriptions—which cluttered the depots had been swept together into battalions which had arbitrarily been labelled as belonging to regiments already serving in Spain and packed off as reinforcements for the great offensive to be launched against Wellington. Unmilitary bodies they were : some hundreds of untrained boys, a dozen officers scraped up from here and from there, a few sergeants from the depot. What little they knew about soldiering had been acquired in the long, long march from France to Portugal, during skirmishes with Spanish guerillas and Portuguese irregulars and British outposts. At the one pitched battle, Busaco, this unhappy Eighth Corps had been kept discreetly in the background while Ney had led the veterans of the other Corps to red ruin against the British line.

They had never known as yet the kindly sensation of being included in a regiment, a properly constituted regiment with staff and transport and efficient officers. The half-dozen pack-mules they had been allotted had broken down months ago on the heartbreaking mountain roads of Spain. Even the battalion papers and accounts—those masses of notes so dear to the French official mind—had vanished. Even the *cantinière* which every self-respecting French unit could boast had deserted them. She had gone off to some other unit which was more experienced and could be relied upon to steal a mule for her when necessary and protect it—and her dubious virtue—from the assaults of hostile irregulars. The fourth battalion of the Forty-Sixth owned nothing, literally nothing, which had not been carried into Portugal on the backs of its aged officers or its eighteen-year-old privates. Since leaving France it had depended for its food on what it could gleam from a harried countryside, and it had cooked it by the light of nature supplemented by the instruction of its half-dozen overworked sergeants. Small wonder, therefore, that of eight hundred men who had entered Spain only six hundred had entered Portugal and only five hundred had lived to assemble in the little village.

The colonel roused himself from his contemplative langour long enough to issue orders for the village and the fields to be swept clear of food which was to constitute a regimental reserve—even his lack-lustre eyes had brightened at the words 'regimental reserve', because the battalion had never owned a reserve of food apart from the bundles of 'cash' which dangled from the men's belts. And yet when it was all brought in and the men had lived on it for a couple of days little enough remained. Five hundred starving men can eat all that is to be found in a little village when the villagers have had time to make their escape. There was a little heap of potatoes, and a sack or two of corn scraped from the corners of the barn, and that was all. In a couple of days' time the battalion would be back again in its normal state of semi-starvation, unless, miraculously, the headquarters which seemed to care so little should do something about it.

The colonel roused himself again. Twice he sent out a company across the high road, and each time by good luck they came back with food. Once they caught a little girl herding sheep, and took all her flock and left her weeping. An older regiment would have given her, young as she was, something more to weep over. Once they found a solitary farm, deserted, and found much corn and maize there, so that the whole foraging party was not merely able to load itself but also filled a cart with the food which they dragged back by hand to the village. But all this only managed to stave off starvation for a day or two. Five hundred men eat an enormous bulk of food every day. Even twenty sheep do not go very far among five hundred men. And they loathed the corn ration. The mill beyond the road had been burnt, and the men could only pound their corn between two rocks and then boil the product into a sort of porridge which revolted the stomach after the fifth meal.

And when it came round to the turn of Sergeant Godinot's company to go out foraging beyond the high road there was an unpleasant surprise awaiting them. They encountered a column of troops before they had marched five miles—French troops, hard-bitten veterans of Reynier's Second Corps. The officer in command of the newcomers halted his men and rode up to the company. The men heard every word of the dialogue between him and the captain.

'What are you doing here? Foraging?'

'Yes,' said the captain.

'You have no right here. The general order gave us this area for foraging.'

'But we must—the battalion has nothing.'

'You must not. I will not have it. We need all we can find here for ourselves. Take your miserable recruits away out of my district.'

The captain refused to be browbeaten.

'I have orders from my colonel to forage here. I insist upon going on.'

'You insist, do you?'

The colonel turned and bawled an order to his waiting battalion. There was a long ripple of steel down the line as they fixed bayonets.

'Now, sir,' said the colonel, 'please do not waste any more of my time or my men's. I mean every word I say. Take your blues away out of my district.'

The men of the Second Corps—veterans of Austerlitz, who had fought in four campaigns

96

in Spain—would use their bayonets on their own fathers if it came to a question of food—and both sides knew it. All that the captain could say was that his colonel would protest to headquarters about this outrage.

'He can protest as much as he likes,' shrugged the colonel. 'Meanwhile my Captain Gauthier will escort you back to the high road just in case you are thinking of looking for another way into my territory after leaving us. Good day to you, captain.'

All that the company could do was to march back with their tails between their legs, while oaths rippled along the ranks—oaths which were re-echoed when the rest of the battalion in the village turned out to welcome them on their return and heard the news that they had come back empty-handed. They saw the captain after making his report ride off on the colonel's horse—the only animal the battalion possessed—and they saw him come back late in the day dejected and unhappy. Headquarters had confirmed the order regarding the foraging area allotted to the fourth battalion of the Forty-Sixth.

Still, there remained the mountain by the river for them to seek food upon—not a very hopeful prospect, apparently, at sight of the rocks and gullies which was all it seemed to consist of. Next morning four companies were paraded to search the mountain. There were little, straggling paths winding here and there up the mountain side, goat tracks where men could walk in single file.

'We ought to find goats up here,' grumbled Lebrun, slipping and stumbling as he made his way up the path behind Godinot. 'They are the only creatures who could live here.'

'Goats will be good enough for me,' said Bernhard the optimist. 'A nice collop of goat, with onions.'

'The people we chased away when we first came here must be somewhere near,' said Dubois, joining in the conversation. 'And their sheep and their cattle. I would rather have a beefsteak than any collop of goat.'

'Beefsteak! Listen to that man!' said Lebrun. 'Served on silver, I suppose, by attentive naked damsels?'

'That would be better,' agreed Dubois.

Somewhere ahead they heard a musket shot, beyond the head of the long, straggling column.

'That's one of Dubois' damsels,' said Lebrun. 'Out with her blunderbuss. She wants a collop of Frenchman for dinner today.'

The column still pushed on up the path. Occasionally a shot or two sounded at the head of the column. After a while they passed a dead man lying at the side of the path—a dead Frenchman, with a blue hole in his forehead and his brains running out on to the heather. Lebrun made no joke about him.

Then word was passed down the line for

Sergeant Godinot's section to take the path to the right, and the order had no sooner reached them than they reached the path named— another goat track diverging from the one up which the company was advancing. Godinot led his twenty men up the path. Away to their left they could hear the rest of the company still stumbling and climbing up the slope, but they had not gone twenty yards before they could no longer see them, so broken was the hillside and so thick the undergrowth.

'I was right about my goats,' muttered Lebrun, pointing to the ground.

'Goats be damned!' said Fournier. 'That's sheep, man. Sheep! Stewed mutton for dinner!'

There were sheep's footprints and sheep's dung all along the path, and the men pressed forward eagerly.

There was more firing away to the left. Godinot strove to see what was happening there, but he could see nothing at all. Then a shot or two were heard to the right; clearly the battalion was extended over the hill, but still they could see nothing, neither friends nor enemies. Now the path through the bushes began to descend. It was no fortuitous dip, either : the descent was too prolonged and too steep for that. At one corner they had a glimpse of the wide, green Tagus below them, before a turn in the path hid it again from view. Then they went on down the descent until the river came in view again, closer this time. And in the end the path ceased abruptly at the water's edge, and Godinot and his men looked at each other.

'The sheep seem to have found another way round, sergeant,' said Fournier.

'We'll find them all the same,' said Godinot. 'Up this path, boys.'

They turned their backs on the river and plunged up the hill again. Right ahead of them they heard more firing. Godinot halted his men and listened carefully. It seemed as if they must have penetrated the enemy's skirmishing line by some unguarded gap. They must be in the rear of the Portuguese. Then they heard a shot from close ahead. Godinot beckoned to Fournier and Bernhard and the three of them crept cautiously forward, leaving the others behind. They tried to move silently up the stony path and through the thorny undergrowth. They heard something moving ahead of them, and crouched silently by the path. Then someone came running down towards them. Godinot gathered his limbs under him and sprang, and he and the man upon whom he had leaped fell with a crash on the path. Fournier and Bernhard came up to them and helped secure the prisoner—an old Portuguese peasant, very old, very wrinkled. His face was like an old potato, brown and lumpy. And it was as expressionless as a potato too. He crouched while the Frenchmen stood round him, gazing before him without moving a feature. They dragged him back to where the rest of the section awaited them.

'Get out and scout,' said Godinot. 'You, and you, and you.'

Three of the men seized their muskets and plunged up and down the path to guard against surprise while Godinot turned to the prisoner, raking through his mind for the few words of Portuguese which he had picked up. He turned to ask for food, for sheep, for cattle, for corn.

'*Alimento*,' said Godinot, bending over the prisoner. '*Ovelha. Gado. Gãro.*'

The prisoner said nothing; he merely sat on his haunches gazing out into infinity. Godinot repeated himself; still the prisoner said nothing. Godinot set his teeth and cocked his musket, and thrust the muzzle against the peasant's ear.

'*Alimento*,' said Godinot.

The prisoner drew a long shuddering breath, but otherwise he made no sound.

'*Alimento*,' said Godinot again, jogging the man's head with his musket barrel, but it was still unavailing.

'Here,' said somebody. 'I'll do it, sergeant. Where are those sheep, curse you?'

The man's bayonet was fixed; he stuck an inch of the point into the peasant's arm and twisted it. This time a groan escaped the prisoner's lips, but he said nothing articulate.

'That's enough,' snapped Godinot, his gorge rising. 'We'll take him back with us. Bring him along.'

Someone fastened the man's wrists behind him, and, dragging him with them, they climbed the path. So broken and overgrown was the hillside that they could see nothing of the rest of the battalion, and it was only with difficulty that they found their way over the hill back to the village, where the old man gazed broken-hearted at the ruin the invaders had caused.

The sergeant-major, Adjutant Doguereau, was overjoyed at their appearance.

'A prisoner, sergeant? Excellent! He will tell us where his food is hidden.'

'He would tell me nothing,' said Godinot.

Doguereau glared down at the old man, who had collapsed at Godinot's feet. Blood was still dripping from his sleeve where the bayonet had pricked him.

'Indeed?' said Doguereau. 'I expect he will tell *me*. Me and Sergeant Minguet.'

Adjutant Doguereau had served in Egypt; he knew something about making prisoners talk. His swarthy face was twisted into a bitter smile.

'Bring him along to the prison and then tell Sergeant Minguet to report to me there.'

Sergeant Godinot never knew what Adjutant Doguereau and Sergeant Minguet did to the old man in the cottage room which had been set aside as a prison; nor did anyone else, because Doguereau turned out from it the two soldiers undergoing punishment there before he set to work. But the battalion heard the old man scream pitifully, like a child.

And later in the day Doguereau called for Sergeant Godinot and a working party, and came out of the prison dragging the old man with him. The prisoner found difficulty in walking, but he led them out of the village to the fields, and there he indicated a pile of rubbish at one corner.

'Dig here,' said Doguereau.

The working party fell to and swept away the rubbish. Underneath was a board flooring, and when that was pulled up a treasure indeed was revealed. The funnel-shaped silo pit beneath was full of maize, heaps and heaps of it, and when they began to rake that away there were jars of olive oil underneath.

'Take all this to the regimental store,' said Doguereau, rubbing his hands.

'And what about the prisoner, mon adjutant?' asked Godinot. The poor old man was lying by the pit, his face wet with tears. 'Shall we let him go?'

'No, not a bit of it. Take him back to the prison. I expect he will find more yet to tell us later on when I attend to him again.'

But the old man never did reveal any other hidden stores, for he hanged himself in his cell that night.

There was rejoicing in the battalion. Besides the ton of maize which had been found, and the gallons of oil, another section ranging the hillside had found four head of cattle hidden in a gully, although they had not found the person minding them. Altogether there were provisions for the whole five hundred men for nearly a week, and for that it was well worth having a man killed and two wounded in the ambushes on the hill.

CHAPTER TWELVE

During the days that followed Adjutant Doguereau had working parties all over the village and the fields looking for further hidden supplies. They pulled every pile of rubbish and rock to pieces, they probed the floors of the cottages and the edges of the fields, they hunted everywhere, but unavailingly. When provisions were beginning to run short again Doguereau issued orders that another prisoner must be taken. Various small expeditions had been pushed across the mountain top, without success. The peasants who had taken shelter there had grown too cunning, apparently; and no one had ever yet succeeded in finding where their central place of concealment might be.

'All that is no use,' said Adjutant

Doguereau. 'If we want to catch a man we must employ other methods. I want parties of five or six men to go up to the hill at night, and hide there. When morning comes someone will fall into your hands, mark my words. Act intelligently.'

So that midnight found Sergeant Godinot and a small party creeping up the hill, feeling their way up the path as silently as they might, and hiding in the undergrowth when they had penetrated far into the tangled summit. It rained heavily that night—it always seemed to be raining now—and a cold wind blew. They huddled together in the darkness for warmth, not daring to speak lest someone should overhear them. They were all friends together, these men, Sergeant Godinot and his particular intimates, Fournier and Dubois and Lebrun and Bernhard, and two more from his section, Catrin and Guimblot.

When morning came it was, perhaps, inevitable that Godinot should be dissatisfied with the position he had taken up in the darkness. It was not a good ambush : it did not overlook the goat track properly and it did not offer sufficient concealment. What Godinot wanted was some position at an intersection of paths, giving a double chance of making a capture. He got his men together and moved up the path again, every man stooping to keep concealed, and creeping up the stony hill as quietly as they might. They ranged over the hill for some time, seeing nothing, hearing nothing. It was hard to find the perfect ambush. They began to feel that they had been sent out on a fool's errand, although they realized that twenty parties like theirs were out on the hill, and it would be a fortunate chance if in a day one single prisoner were caught. They were only young French soldiers; they had not the patience to lie in the cold rain waiting for their opportunity; they had to move about and seek it.

And the result was perhaps inevitable. There were others on the hill who knew the paths and the contours far better than they, and who could move more silently, and more swiftly. The Frenchmen had come to lay an ambush; instead they walked into one. Sergeant Godinot for the rest of his life felt a feeling of shame when he remembered it—the stupidity with which he had led his party to their death, the panic which overwhelmed him in the moment of danger. A high shelf of rock overlooked the path here, and it was from the shelf that death leaped out at them. There was a crashing, stunning volley and a billow of smoke, and through the smoke the enemy came leaping down at them. Men fell at Godinot's left hand, and at his right. Someone screamed. Two impressions remained printed on Godinot's memory—one of Guimblot coughing up floods of blood at his feet, another of the wild charge of the enemy with the green Englishman at their head, bayonets flashing and smoke eddying. Someone turned and ran, and Godinot ran too, down the path and as he began to run panic gripped him and he ran faster and ever faster, stumbling over the stones, tearing his clothes on the thorns, running so madly that pursuit dropped behind and in the end he was able to slow down and try to recover his breath and his wits.

Dubois was with him. He was wounded, as he said stupidly over and over again—a bullet had gone through his arm. Fournier came up a moment later brandishing his musket.

'I fired at him again,' said Fournier, 'but I missed him clean. He is hard to hit, that one.'

'Where are the others?' asked Godinot. He knew the answer to the question, but he asked it merely for something to say.

'Dead,' said Fournier. 'They shot Bernhard through the heart. Guimblot—'

'I saw Guimblot,' said Godinot.

They looked at each other. Godinot was ashamed of his panic.

'They're coming! They're coming again!' said Dubois, seizing Godinot's arm. A twig snapped somewhere in the undergrowth, and the noise started the panic in their minds again—perhaps it was Dubois' fault, for he was shaken by his wound and panic is infectious. They fled over the hill again, running madly along the paths, until Dubois fainted with loss of blood. They tied up his wound and dragged him down to the village. There was an unpleasant interview with his captain awaiting Sergeant Godinot when he had to explain the loss of more than half his party. There is no excuse for defeat in the military code, just as success excuses everything. But other parties had sustained loss and defeat, too, it appeared, when they came back in driblets from the mountain; there were several wounded to bear Dubois company in the hospital; there were several dead left among the rocks. And several men had seen the Englishman in green uniform, and several shots had been fired at him, all unavailingly.

In the evening Fournier came to Sergeant Godinot.

'I want some money, sergeant,' he said. 'Give me some.' Sergeant Godinot could see no use for money here in these uninhabited billets, and he said so.

'Never mind that,' said Fournier. 'I want some money.'

Godinot bowed to his whim and pulled out two or three copper coins—enough to buy a drink had there been drinks to be bought. Fournier thrust them aside.

'I want *money*,' he said.

What he was really asking for, as Godinot came to realize, was silver—in French the same word. Godinot found him a Spanish pillar dollar, one of four which Godinot kept sewn in his shirt in case of need. Fournier weighed it in his hand.

'Give me another one, sergeant. Please give me another one,' he pleaded.

Godinot did so with some reluctance, looking at him oddly. It was only later in the evening, when he saw Fournier sitting by the fire with an iron spoon and a bullet-mould that he realized part of what was in Fournier's mind. He was casting silver bullets to make sure of hitting the green Englishman at the next opportunity. The others round the fire were not given the chance by Fournier of seeing exactly what he was doing. They made jokes about shortage of ammunition and Fournier's diligence in replacing it, but they did not know it was silver he was using, and in consequence paid no special attention to his actions. After all, bullet-moulding was a pleasantly distracting hobby, and men who were really fussy about their marksmanship were often known to mould their own bullets in an endeavour to obtain more perfect spheres than the official issue.

Yet Sergeant Godinot felt much more ill at ease when at next morning's parade Private Fournier was found to be missing. Everyone realized that it could not be a case of desertion—no one could desert to the Portuguese, and to have deserted to the English would have called for a journey through the cantonments of half the French army. Sergeant Godinot could only tell his captain what he knew of Fournier's motives, and express the opinion that he was out on the hill somewhere trying to shoot the green Englishman. And the captain could only shrug his shoulders and hope that Fournier would return alive.

He never did. Godinot awaited him anxiously for several days, but he never came back. Godinot never found out what happened to him. He was the fifth of that little group of friends to die—Boyel had been the first, and little Godron the second, and Lebrun and Bernhard had been killed in the ambush a day or two before, and now Fournier was gone and only Dubois was left, with a hole in his arm.

So one day after an announcement by the colonel, Sergeant Godinot came to visit Dubois in the battalion hospital.

'We are going to Santarem tomorrow,' said Godinot.

'Who is?'

'We are. You and I. We are going carpentering or rope-making or boat-building—they want men for all those.'

'Who does?'

'Headquarters. The colonel announced this morning that all men with a knowledge of carpentry or boat-building or rope-making or smith's work were to report to the adjutant. So I reported for you and me. I didn't have to tell him more than the truth. When I said that my father owned one-third of the Chantier Naval, and that you and I had spent half our lives in small boats in Nantes harbour, he put our names down at once. We are to report at Santarem tomorrow.'

'Santarem?' asked Dubois vaguely.

'Santarem is twenty kilometres down the river,' said Godinot. 'Heaven bless us, man, don't you remember marching up through it?'

But since the conscription had taken him from his home a year ago, at the age of seventeen and a half, Dubois had marched through too many places to remember half of them.

'So that arm of yours must be better by tomorrow,' said Godinot. 'Half a bullet ought not to keep you sick longer than that.'

The missile which had been extracted from Dubois' arm had been half a musket ball— apparently the Portuguese sawed their bullets in two in order to double their chances of hitting something.

'It is better,' said Dubois. 'I was to report for light duty the day after tomorrow. Do you think they'll issue rations to us at Santarem?'

'They'll have to if we're doing other work,' said Godinot, and the two of them looked at each other. Food was already short again in the battalion—that day's ration had only consisted of a litre of maize porridge. 'It's headquarters at Santarem,' he continued. 'Those brutes in the Second Corps will have to send in some of the beef they get beyond the road.'

Everyone in the battalion was firmly convinced that the Second Corps in its foraging area beyond the road was revelling in beef every day—an extraordinarily inaccurate estimate. Dubois smacked his lips.

'Beef!' he said. 'With thick gravy!'

He said the words with the same respectful awe he had once employed in speaking about the Emperor Napoleon.

Adjutant Doguereau had weeded out a great many of the applicants for work at Santarem. Quite half the battalion had hurried to report to him after the regimental announcement, full of stories about their knowledge of carpentry or rope-making. Everyone was anxious to escape from the battalion, from the dreariness of life in cramped billets, the shortage of food, the endless, ineffectual skirmishing with the outcasts on the hill.

They had told the most fantastic lies about their experience with boats and their ability to do smith's work. But Adjutant Doguereau had seen through all the lies of these lads fresh from the plough and the cart's tail. There were only thirty men paraded under Sergeant Godinot and sent off to march down the road to Santarem.

Santarem was a long, narrow town of tall, white houses squeezed in between the road and the river. When they marched into it there was no sign of civilian life—every inhabitant had fled weeks ago—but the long, high street was all a-bustle with groups of men working here and there. The red woollen shoulder-knots of the engineers were much in evidence. They saw white-haired old General Éblé, whom everyone knew and liked, striding stiffly along the road followed by his staff. A sergeant of sappers took them in charge and led them to their billet—a big warehouse on the water's edge.

'Here, you blues,' cried the sergeant of sappers, 'is where you will live for the next month or two. And where you will work. My God, how you will work!'

'But what is the work, sergeant?' asked Godinot.

'We are going to build a bridge to cross the river. A pontoon bridge. And after that we are going to build another bridge. That makes two.'

Godinot looked out of the open warehouse door, across the quay, to where the river rolled in its green immensity. Two pontoon bridges to cross that width of rushing water—bridges capable of bearing artillery—would be an immense task.

'Yes, you can look,' said the sergeant of sappers. 'The calculation is that we shall need two hundred pontoons. And some pontoons will need four anchors, some only two. And we shall need about ten kilometres of cable for the anchors and the roadway. And the roadway, as you see, will be about a kilometre and a half long for the two bridges. That will have to be made of timber.'

'Have you got the timber and anchors and things?' asked Godinot, a little bewildered.

'No,' said the sergeant. 'But we have a good many houses in the town. We are to pull the houses down and use the joists. And we shall have to save the nails when we pull the houses down because we have no nails. And before we start pulling the houses down we shall have to make the tools to do it with, because we have no tools except a few hammers we have got from the farriers. But there is plenty of iron in the balconies. We have got to make hammers and saws and axes and adzes out of that. And of course we have no hemp for the cables. We have got to make cables. There are three warehouses full of bales of wool. We have got to try if woollen ropes will suit, and it not— well, we have got to try ropes made of linen, or hay, or straw, or we shall have to tie together every odd bit of rope the army can find in its billets. And there is no tar, of course, for the bottoms of the pontoons. I don't think General Éblé has thought of a way round the difficulty of the tar. There is olive oil, however. Is there anyone here who knows how to make a durable paint out of olive oil? I thought not. But they have begun experiments already down the road. If you sniff attentively you may be able to smell them.'

This long speech by the sergeant of sappers was received with a chilly silence by his audience. The French recruit takes none of the delight in extemporization which his counterpart across the Channel displays. This talk of building bridges to cross a half-mile river out of floor-joists appeared to their minds to take far too much for granted. The sergeant of sappers knew it, but he could do nothing in the matter except change the subject.

'Five o'clock,' he said. 'Too late to start work today. Report with your party at five o'clock tomorrow morning, sergeant.'

Godinot instantly broached the subject which lay nearest to their hearts.

'What about rations, sergeant?' he asked.

'Rations? *Rations*? Do you blues mean to say you want *rations*? I don't know why you have come to Santarem, then. You must hurry to the quartermaster's store and see what there is. They served out the day's rations an hour ago.'

'What was it, sergeant?' asked Dubois.

'Maize,' said the sergeant of sappers. 'Unground maize. One pound per man. That is what they were issuing an hour ago. There may be some left, but I doubt it.'

As it happened, the doubts of the sergeant of sappers were ill-founded. Every man in Sergeant Godinot's party received his pound of maize. It only remained for them to pound it as well as they could, and then boil it into porridge over a fire made of what wood they could steal. It constituted a poor day's food for men engaged in hard physical work.

CHAPTER THIRTEEN

Life among the outcasts in the rocky mountain by the river settled down extraordinarily quickly into routine. The Portuguese peasants had been accustomed all their lives to unremitting hard work, and gladly took up what labour there was to be done—it irked them to be idle. So that it was quite willingly that they did sentry-go along the brow of the hill, and slaved to enlarge the cave by the river so that there might be shelter in it for all. It was the women's task to look after the cattle on the hill and move them from point to point so that they might find herbage here and there—scanty herbage, but enough to keep them just alive. The constant fear of attack by the French kept everyone from quarrelling.

It was all very matter-of-fact and obvious. When shots from the brow of the hill told that an attack was developing there, everyone knew what he had to do. The little flock of sheep was driven down to the river's brink and carried one by one on the backs of men and women over the secret ford to the little beach outside the cave. The women drove the large cattle into hidden gullies and left them there, perforce, while they came down for shelter to the caves as well. The men took their muskets and went out on the hillside to skirmish with the enemy. There was ample time for everything to be done, because on the precipitous goat tracks through the rocks and the undergrowth the French soldiers moved so slowly that an interval hours long occurred between the firing of the first warning shots and the arrival of the French anywhere where they might be dangerous.

The very first attack, made only a few days after the arrival of the French, was perhaps the most successful. It was only a short while after daybreak that a musket shot told of the danger, and Dodd had seized his rifle, and, with Bernardino at his side, had hurried to the broad flat rock on the summit which the peasants called 'the table' to see what was developing.

It was the usual sort of attack—four columns of men pushing up the hill by perilous goat tracks through the bush. Dodd could catch glimpses of each in turn making the slow ascent whenever the conformation of the ground brought them into view. Each column consisted of a company; even at that distance he could see in the clear air that one column wore the bearskins of the grenadiers of the battalion and another the plumes of the *voltigeurs*—'light bobs' Dodd called them mentally; the remaining two companies of the battalion had been left behind, of course, to act as head-quarters guard. The progress of the attackers was inordinately slow. They had continually to halt to enable the rear to catch up with the head. The three sentries who had given the alarm were able to slip round by other paths and take long shots into the caterpillars of men crawling up the slope. Dodd and the other half-dozen men who gathered round him had ample time to choose their course of action and glide along the crest away to the flank and by heavy firing there bring one of the columns to a complete stop.

Yet it was a damaging day. The other columns had broken into smaller parties, which had ranged very thoroughly over the top of the mountain—as thoroughly, that is to say, as twelve small parties could range over an immense hilltop seamed and broken with gullies. One such party must have found the cattle, the four draught bullocks who had drawn the village plough in the days before the French came. And perhaps another such party had found Miguel. However it was, Miguel was missing. He might be dead, and his body might be lying somewhere out on the hillside. No one knew what had become of old Miguel, and the women in the cave that night wept for him— more bitterly, perhaps, than the men bewailed the loss of the draught oxen. They sought him next day over the hill without finding him, but later in the day one of the watchers on the brow of the hill came in with news of him.

He had seen Miguel brought out of the village and buried by the fields; he was sure it was Miguel, even at that distance. The French must have dragged him into the village and murdered him. There was more wailing among the women. Miguel had led a solitary life lately; his wife was dead and his sons had been conscripted into the army, but everyone in that village was related to everyone else; they had intermarried for generations, even (as was not unusual in those lost villages) within the prohibited degrees. Miguel was mourned by cousins and nieces and daughters-in-law.

The other information which the watchers on the hill brought, to the effect that the French had discovered the hidden stores of food in Miguel's silo, went almost unnoticed in the general dismay.

Nevertheless, Miguel's death was not long unavenged. There came a morning when Bernardino, flushed with excitement, came hurriedly to Dodd and the others and led them to 'the table', where they gathered with infinite caution. Bernardino pointed down the hill, and everyone followed his gesture. Far down the slope they could see half a dozen men crawling along a path. They were bent double, and moving with such ludicrous care that

Bernardino could not help giggling as he pointed to them: it was so amusing to see them picking their way with so much caution and ignorant that they had been observed.

It was Dodd who laid the ambush. He guessed the future route of the little party, and brought his men hurriedly across the slope to where they could await their arrival unseen. He had lain on his stomach with his rifle pushed out in front of him ready for action, and the others had imitated him. And, when at one point of their course the Frenchmen had shown up clearly and just within range, he had turned his head and had glowered at his men with such intensity that they had restrained their natural instincts and had not fired, but had waited instead for the better opportunity which Dodd had foreseen.

The volley at ten yards and the instant charge which Dodd had headed had been effective enough. There were three men dead and another one wounded, whose throat Pedro had cut the instant Dodd's back was turned, and the survivors had fled down the path as though the devil was behind them. Dodd would have been glad if they had all been killed, but to kill seven men with a volley from seven muskets even at ten yards was much more than could be expected—a pity, all the same, for Dodd could guess at the moral effect it would have had on the battalion if a whole detachment had been cut off without trace.

He had forbidden pursuit, calling back Bernardino who had begun to run down the path after the fugitives. There was no sense in running madly about the hill where other enemies were to be found; there might indeed be danger.

Instead, Dodd made the best move possible in taking his men back to 'the table' and scanning the hill for further parties of the enemy, and when he saw none he pushed out scouts here and there to seek for them. Two other little groups were located during the day, and Dodd brought up his men to attack them, creeping cautiously through the undergrowth. But neither attack was as successful as the first—the first burst of firing had set them on the alert and it had not been possible to approach them closely. They could only follow them back to the village in a long, straggling fight in which very much powder was expended and very few people hurt—several of the Portuguese received flesh wounds.

All the same, it had been a glorious day. The new French plan of pushing small parties up the hill under cover of darkness had been heavily defeated. And every man on the hill now had a good French musket and bayonet and ammunition. taken from the corpses of the slain.

Next day there was a stranger incident, which Dodd never fully understood. It was quite late in the afternoon when Dodd, crossing the hill with Bernardino at his heels, felt a bullet whiz by his face, and heard the crack of a musket from the bushes to his right. He dropped instantly to the ground, and peered in the direction whence the shot had come. A wisp of smoke still drifting through the bushes indicated clearly enough the position of the man who had missed so narrowly. Whether there was one man there or twenty Dodd did not know. He crawled to cover behind a rock and sighted his rifle carefully on the neighbourhood of the hiding-place of the enemy.

Bernardino began to crawl like a snake up the path again—perhaps to turn the enemy's flank, perhaps to direct the attack of the other defenders of the hill who would be attracted to the spot by the firing.

Dodd gazed along the barrel of his rifle. Soon he saw the bushes in movement, and he knew what was moving them—he had played this game so often before. Someone there was trying to reload his musket; it was a terribly difficult thing to do when lying down trying to keep concealed. Dodd did his best to judge by the amount of movement the position of the head and feet of the man who was loading. Then he sighted for the mid-point between them and fired, instantly rolling behind his rock again. No shot came in reply. Dodd wriggled on his belly away from his rock, down the path, until a journey of twenty yards brought him to a dip in the ground which promised complete concealment. Here, lying on his back, he contrived to reload. Fortunately on this occasion the bullet did not jam in the rifling, but slid sweetly down to rest on the wadding. He laid the weapon down beside his head, rolled over on his stomach, and took hold of it again. Then he wriggled away to another rock from which he could bring under observation the area of scrub into which he had fired.

He pushed his rifle forward and took aim, but he could see no sign of movement. His straining ears could just detect the sound of someone creeping through the bush higher up, but that was doubtless Bernardino—it came from his direction. Dodd lay very still, with all his senses on the alert, scanning the thick bushes all round for any sign of an enemy— they might not all be in the same spot; they might be creeping upon him from any point of the compass. With dreadful patience he lay still. His ears actually twitched, so tensely was he tuned up, when some particularly clumsy movement on Bernardino's part made more noise than usual.

Then, at the end of a very long time, he saw far out to his right the top of an English infantry shako appear above the bushes. That was Bernardino, employing the age-old trick of raising his hat on a stick to draw the enemy's fire. It was specially useful in this case, because it told Dodd where Bernardino was. With the knowledge that that flank was secure, he was able to assume the offensive. He set his rifle at half-cock—Dodd was far too careful a man to crawl through undergrowth with a cocked rifle—and began another very cautious advance. He writhed along through the bushes, raising no part of himself off the ground, using his toes and his elbows, moving inches at a time at the cost of prodigious exertion.

At last the time came when he could see his enemy—a part of him, at least. He could see the top of a black gaiter and a bit of the leg of a pair of extremely dirty white breeches. Change his position as he might within moderate limits, he could bring no other part of the enemy into view as a result of the lie of the land. He took careful aim at the knee of the breeches, and fired. He was sure he had hit the mark; he thought he saw the leg leap before the smoke obscured his view, but when he looked again the leg was still lying there. Once again, after carefully moving away from where he had fired, Dodd performed the difficult contortionist's feat of loading while lying down. Then he writhed forward again in a narrowing arc. He put his hat on his ramrod, and holding it at arm's length, raised it above the bushes. It drew no fire, and, after a time, the signal was answered by Bernardino from a position right in his front. They had turned both flanks of the enemy on a wide curve, apparently. There could be no one else near save whoever it was—be it few or many—at the point whence the first shot had been fired. Dodd began to suspect the truth of the matter, but he was far too cautious and patient to risk his life by a rash testing of his suspicions. He resumed his tedious, difficult advance, creeping through the scrub, changing his direction every yard or so to avoid having to crawl over some lump of rock which might lift him an inch or two above the skyline.

At last he reached the position of the enemy, and found that his suspicions were correct. There had only been one man there all the time, and Dodd had killed him with his first shot. The bullet had hit him in the groin, and, bursting the great artery of the thigh, had drained the life out of him in twenty seconds. He lay tranquil on his left side in the midst of a great pool of congealed blood. Only a few drops of blood had trickled from his other wound in his right knee which must have been inflicted after death.

Bernardino, when he arrived a few seconds later, was intensely amused that they had expended so much time and energy on stalking a dead man. But he displayed admiration at the fact that Dodd had hit his man twice with two shots, both of them at a range of over fifty yards. The dead man lay on his left side. His ramrod was in his right hand, clearly indicating that he had been killed while reloading. His left hand was clenched, but when Bernardino turned him over to go through his pockets something fell from it—the bullet which he had been about to ram into his musket.

It did not have the usual dull grey colour. It had a bright, frosted appearance. Dodd picked it up idly. It was not as heavy as usual; it did not seem to be a leaden bullet. Dodd fancied, but he could not believe it, that it must be a silver one. He could not believe it to be silver; he came to the conclusion that the French must be running short of ammunition and casting bullets out of scrap metal. He tossed it away idly into the bushes.

That was not the only puzzling item in the business. The dead man must have lain hidden there for a long time—since before dawn of that day, most probably. He must almost for certain have had opportunities of shooting at several other people before Dodd came in range. There was no obvious reason at all why he had come alone into the enemy's territory, nor yet why, having come here, he should have waited to fire at Dodd in particular. Dodd simply could not understand it. He had never heard of the superstition that to kill a very important person, or one with diabolical powers, a silver bullet is desirable. Modestly, he could not imagine—it never came within the farthest possibility of occurring to him— that he might have come to bulk so large in poor Fournier's tortured imagination. Dodd gave up puzzling about the business once he had decided that it had no important bearing upon his own welfare and that of his followers. No one else of the party seemed to give the matter a second thought, as far as Dodd could ascertain. It was merely one more Frenchman dead, another little step in the right direction. They turned from the death of this Frenchman to planning the death of the next.

So day succeeded day. Still the battalion huddled in its overcrowded cottages and outhouses down in the village, and still the Portuguese starved and shivered on the hill. There were days and nights of torrential, drenching rain and bitter winds, which largely explained the inactivity of the French. There was spasmodic starvation in the village, and more ordered starvation on the hill. Dodd had begun to guess that the French were going to stay where they were until privation drove them out. It would be a starving match, and he wanted to see that his side could starve longest. The precious flour and corn were hoarded religiously, even though the damp had begun to make them mouldy. The five cows were killed and eaten first—it was hard to feed them and there was always the danger that the enemy might capture them in some new attack on the hill. Then the sheep were eaten, beginning first with the ones which died of starvation and exposure. The Portuguese grew restless under this diet of unrelieved meat—they were never great eaters of that commodity at any time. They clamoured for bread, but Dodd set his face resolutely against their demands and old Maria, who had taken charge of the stores at the end of the cave, backed him up. She seemed wiser than the others, and met all their demands for bread and for cakes fried in oil with a resolute '*Não, não*' whose nasal tones seemed to voice all her contempt for the masculine half of humanity in every branch of human activity, from housekeeping to planning a campaign—although in this kind of warfare those two particular objectives were not specially distinct.

The wretched peasants, of course, saw utter ruin ahead of them. Their fields were being left untilled, their buildings were being mined, and now they were being compelled to eat their livestock without leaving any nucleus at all which might multiply in the years to come. The score or so of diseased and starving sheep which were carried twice daily across the secret ford represented now their sole wealth; when that was gone they would have nothing, literally nothing. They would starve whether the French retreated or whether the French stayed. Yet it was not a matter in which any principle could be debated except for the small details, because there was always one great outstanding fact—it would mean far more certain death to yield to the French now than to stay up here in the mountain and starve. Everyone remembered the fate of Miguel.

Dodd by now could understand a little of all this which was being said around him. He had to learn the language as a child learns his native tongue. When Dodd used a noun and a verb and made a sentence out of them he had not the least consciousness of these three operations; he did not know what was a noun or a verb, or a sentence. Being unable to read or write naturally made learning difficult for him. He progressed eventually into the condition of an eighteen-months-old child—he understood most of what was said to him, but all he could employ in reply was a small collection of nouns and verbs which made not the slightest attempt to agree with each other. Yet his prestige never suffered on account of the ludicrous things he said; he was far too adept at killing Frenchmen ever to appear in the least ridiculous in the eyes of the peasants.

CHAPTER FOURTEEN

There was little enough which went on in the village where the fourth battalion of the Forty-Sixth rotted in stagnation which was unobserved by the keen-eyed watchers on the hill. The sentinels saw everything. They could report the continual and most unsuccessful search which went on in the arable land for food. They could see little parties of men—ever armed and vigilant—seeking nettles and edible weeds to add to their meagre diet. They reported whenever a small grudging convoy of food reached the battalion from headquarters—which was not very often. They knew when sickness smote the wretched troops, because they could see sick men staggering up to the hospital-cottage, and they could see the corpses being carried out for burial, and they chuckled over it. Dysentery, it was, the inevitable result of weeks of exposure and bad food. They explained the nature of the disease to Dodd with a vivid explanatory pantomime, and Dodd nodded grimly. There was not a soldier alive who did not know a great deal about dysentery. Bernardino grinned broadly when from the brow of the hill he pointed out how greatly extended were the battalion latrines and how continually crowded they were.

Naturally, Dodd realized, there were no medicines for the French down there; there were no medicines for the whole French army huddled in its billets around Santarem, and there was no means of obtaining any. The hundred and fifty miles of mountain road which lay between the French and the frontier even of Spain were quite blocked by the hordes of starving irregulars whom Wellington had mobilized. Not so much as a letter—far less a convoy—had reached the French since the time, three months back, when they crossed the frontier. In all that time, while conducting sieges, fighting battles and worried by skirmishes innumerable, they had lived on what they could find in a country naturally poor and which had in great part been laid waste before them.

On the only occasion when they had been able to send news of themselves back to France the messenger had been escorted by six hundred men who had had to fight every yard of the road and had left half their numbers by the wayside. Even Dodd, who knew much about the French military capacity, marvelled at the way in which they hung on to their uncomfortable position; Dodd, of course, knew nothing of the fierce determination of the Marshal in command; he had never even heard of the siege of Genoa ten years back, when this same Marshal had defended the town with troops fed on a daily ration of half a pound of hair-powder the while the prisoners he took ate each other because they were given nothing to eat at all. No one could bring himself to believe that the Marshal would try to repeat his exploit, and would hold on until thirty thousand men were dead of disease so that it was dangerous to linger further before an English army making ready to sally out upon them.

Besides, Dodd could not imagine any object

131

at all in this hanging on. He did not know anything about high politics, and so could not appreciate the fact that England was going through a Cabinet crisis which might quite possibly result in the assumption of power by the Opposition and a prompt withdrawal of Wellington from his impregnable position. Nor could he envisage at first the major strategical situation, and grasp the main military reason for this fierce retention of the position along the Tagus. What initiated the train of events which in the end gave him an insight into the matter was the sound of guns down the river.

Faint it was, and yet distinct enough. Dodd, walking in the dawn on the hillside, heard the distant rumble and stopped, listening intently, with his heart beating faster because of the possibilities which the sound implied. It was distinctly the firing of big guns. It was not a big battle—there was not enough gunfire for that. Nor was it a siege, for the firing was in no way continuous. Yet guns were firing, and to Dodd that was terribly important. For it must imply that the French were in contact with the regular enemy not far away. And any enemy of the French must be Dodd's friends; they must be British or Portuguese, and formed troops at that, because of the artillery. If he could only join them he would be back in his regiment almost at once—the regiment, his home. Every good soldier must rally to his regiment.

He listened again to the firing; it was not in

salvos, but he could detect individual shots, and from their loudness he could estimate by experience how far away they were. Certainly not at the Lines—the firing was a good deal nearer than that. What was there down the river a dozen miles away? The only point of any strategical value that he could think of was Santarem, but he was not sure how far off Santarem was. He turned to Bernardino.

'Santarem?' he said. 'Where?'

It took a little while for Bernardino to realize what he was being asked, but he gave the right answer at last. 'Five,' he said, and held up five fingers.

Five Portuguese leagues meant ten miles or a little more; the firing was certainly at Santarem.

'We go,' said Dodd, with decision. He turned back to the cave to make his preparations for the move.

Down in the cave the news that their English leader was about to go to Santarem roused mixed emotions. Some wanted to accompany him; some wanted him to stay. Dodd swept away their arguments with the few words at his disposal. They must stay; there was still food to guard, there was still the battalion to worry. Moreover, he foresaw a dangerous march through the French cantonments. One or two men might slip through where a party of a dozen would be detected. Bernardino must accompany him of course—Dodd could hardly now imagine any risky march through Portugal without Bernardino, and he would be extremely useful to explain matters in the very likely event of encountering any further parties of Portuguese irregulars. Dodd filled his haversack with unleavened bread from the pile Maria was slowly accumulating in the cave— the result of continuous small bakings in a make-shift oven over a screened fire. He strapped on his greatcoat, saw that he had his ammunition and flints, filled his canteen from the river, and was ready. Bernardino had made similar preparations, imitating each of his actions like a monkey. Then they set out, up the steep path, across the stony mountain, and down to where the little lane ran from the village over to the high road.

Caution was necessary here: there might be patrols or sentries or stray parties moving along the lane. They edged cautiously down to the top of the bank, and peered through the rain this way and that. When they were satisfied that it was safe they plunged down the bank, across the lane, and up the other side. They climbed hurriedly until the rocks and bushes gave them cover again.

Now they were on the long, low hill which had been the scene of their first skirmish with the battalion. They picked their way up it cautiously, ready to fall flat at the sight of Frenchmen. But the driving rain was a good screen. They saw no one. Dodd directed his course diagonally over the hill, threading his way through rocks and bushes until once more they were over the Tagus bank. Dodd did not wish to be too far from the river, not so much because of its use as a guide—the high road beyond the hill would have been as useful in that respect—but because he knew instinctively that the river was the most important strategical factor in the situation; that anything which might affect his destiny must, in the present conditions, happen on the river. He gazed down, as he strode along with Bernardino beside him, at the broad, green mass of water pouring sullenly down between its rocky banks, and at the floating stuff which swirled in its eddies.

He had seen a British gunboat pushing its way up here once, but he had no hope of seeing another; he guessed that the French must have established shore batteries down by Alhandra to stop such voyages. Yet at the same time he had a strong suspicion that the gunfire at Santarem must be due to activity on the river by the British forces, though what form that activity was taking he could not imagine. The more he thought about it, the more he hurried his pace without relaxing his strained alertness lest the enemy should appear. The merest possibility that he might find a chance of rejoining his friends was enough to rouse passionate excitement in his breast.

Dodd never stopped to think that perhaps he was doing better work for England out here organizing the irregulars than if he were inside the Lines lost in the ranks of the Ninety-Fifth; that would have been a form of presumption quite foreign to his nature. He knew his place and his duty. England had spent a great deal of money and the deepest thought of her keenest minds on making a good soldier of him; she could have made a useful citizen of him for one-half the expense and trouble if there had been no war—except that in that case she would have judged it better policy to save her money.

The gunfire had largely died away as the day went on; there were only a very few distant reports to mark the fact that the activity at Santarem, whatever the reason for it, still continued to a small extent. It was late afternoon before they came to the end of the hill, where the river came back to the road, and had to stop to consider their next movements. Santarem was not more than four or five miles farther on, but here the plain came down nearly to the river's bank, and only a short distance ahead of them was another little village lying along the main road. A village meant French troops and the need for infinite caution.

Dodd scanned the landscape from the river side of the hill without seeing any safe route

136

for further progress. With the puzzled Bernardino trailing behind him he crossed the hilltop and examined the lie of the land from the side by the main road. Nor from here could he see any means of pushing on: it was level plain land for a great distance, dotted here and there with villages and farm buildings. At more than one point he could see parties of French troops moving along the paths out there. Clearly it would be a dangerous enterprise to try to make his way through that country. Bernardino voiced his disgust at the prospect; he was for turning back again, and a man less obstinate than Dodd might have yielded, or one with a lower ideal of military duty. But the British army had not won the distinction it now possessed by turning back at the first sign of difficulty; nor would Dodd turn back now.

Certainly he did retrace his steps a little way, but that was in search of another way round. Bernardino grumbled bitterly when he realized that Dodd was not turning home-ward, but Dodd paid no attention to his complaints—he only understood one word in twenty of them, anyway. A mile back along the hill the other side of the main road was bordered by a thick wood, stretching inland for some considerable distance. At the farther end of it a view could be obtained which might throw fresh light on the situation. Dodd picked his way cautiously down to the road, scuttled across it when he was sure no Frenchman was in sight, and then plunged into the forest.

It was in the heart of the wood that they found the man who was to help them. The encounter was a surprise to all three of them. They were all making their way cautiously from tree to tree, listening hard for the enemy, when simultaneously they caught a glimpse of each other across a glade. All three of them dived for cover and reached for their weapons instinctively, but Bernardino had had a clear view of the stranger for a tenth of a second, and saw that he wore no uniform. He called to him in Portuguese and received an answer in that language, and, finally, prodded by Dodd, he stood up and moved into the open. That was taking a slight chance, because a hunted Portuguese might possibly fire first and answer questions after, but in this case the move was successful. The other man came forward into the glade, and to explain the situation to him. The stranger was a stunted little man, with a knife at his belt and a musket in his hand; he glanced keenly up and down Dodd's burly form as Bernardino explained the presence of an Englishman. The stranger led them away through the forest, and then on his hands and knees plunged into an insignificant tunnel into a tangle of undergrowth. A few yards farther in, the bushes ceased for a space around the trunk of a great tree, and against the tree was built a little three-sided shelter of twigs and branches. On the ground inside the hut, with a few rags spread over him, lay an old man, with a mop of tangled white hair and beard, moaning and muttering to himself.

'My father,' said the stranger, by way of introduction, and then he knelt beside the pitiful form, trying to give him a little comfort, whispering little words to him as though to a child.

He was dying from one of the diseases of famine or exposure, typhus or plague, or pneumonia—pneumonia, most likely, to judge from his rapid laboured breathing and the fluttering of his nostrils. There were tears in the stunted man's eyes when he backed out of the shelter again and turned to face Dodd and Bernardino; tears which ran down his cheeks and lost themselves among the sparse hairs of his beard.

Bernardino was too young, and had seen too much of war lately, to be much moved by the sight of the illness of an old man who was bound to die rather sooner than later anyway. He explained that Dodd was anxious to see Santarem, to inspect the cause of the gunfire there. The stunted man shook his head, and indicated his father. He said he could not leave him. An argument developed there in the little clearing, while the light faded and the rain dripped dismally among the branches. Dodd played his part in the argument.

'I go Santarem,' he said, and then, his small

vocabulary failing because he did not know the Portuguese for 'cannon' nor for 'see', he looked out under his hand and then said 'Boom, boom'.

The stunted man nodded; Bernardino had already given quite an adequate account of what this Englishman wanted to do. But the stunted man pointed to his father and shook his head. He would not leave his father to act as a guide to them. Bernardino demanded if they could make their way to within sight of Santarem without his guiding them, but the stunted man shook his head again. There were very many Frenchmen in the way. It would be quite impossible. He could take them by night, but no one who did not know the country could hope to get through.

There was nothing for it but to wait for the old man to die; fortunately that did not take long—only thirty-six hours. Dodd and Bernardino helped the son to bury him— Bernardino very sulky and dodging as much of the work as possible. He looked on it as very unnecessary labour and none of his business; but the stunted man wept bitterly, and constantly bewailed the fact that his father had died unshriven, and without a priest to bury him, and with uncounted years of purgatory before him in consequence. Dodd was not much moved, anyway. His trade was in death, and he had seen much of it of late years. He was engaged in war, and war without death was a quite unthinkable thing. And seeing that England had been engaged in one continuous war since he was a child in petticoats a world without war was equally unthinkable. And Dodd had far too much practical commonsense ever to begin to think about such a fantastic notion as a world without the possibility of war. He was far too deeply occupied, moreover, with his present business of killing Frenchmen, or aiding them to starve to death, or tormenting them with disease.

CHAPTER FIFTEEN

When night fell again after they had scooped the shallow grave in the leafmould and had covered up the wasted body and the white hair, they set out again for Santarem. The stunted man had been speaking the truth when he had said that they could not find the way by night without his aid. They crept across several fields, following a zigzag route through the rainy darkness, apparently to make sure of their direction by going from one landmark to another—a tree or a disused plough. At one place the stunted man enjoined special precaution. They could just see him in the darkness lower himself down into a drainage ditch alongside a field, and crept after him along it—there was a trough in the bottom of the ditch and they could walk with one foot on each side of the water. Only thirty yards away they heard the challenge of a sentry and the reply of the visiting rounds—apparently they were creeping past a village. After a long wait they crept along the ditch. Some distance along they emerged, crept across the *pavé* of the road, and plunged into another ditch. Then there was more creeping and crawling. They crossed a field thick with weeds, apparently, and at last they heard the rushing gurgling sound of the Tagus close at hand. Soon they were on its very bank, and could just discern the dark surface of the water. They crept along above the river for a few more yards, and then their guide checked them, and lowered himself with infinite precaution over the edge. They followed him, and, guided by his whispers and sharp pokes from his fingers, they lay down under the edge of the bank. Here the river rose within ten feet of the level of the surrounding country; it had reached its maximum winter level now. The strip of vertical bank still exposed was covered with vegetation dragging out a miserable existence among the rocks—myrtle bushes, Dodd thought. They afforded very fair cover, and here they waited for the dawn, wet and weary. Bernardino's teeth chattered.

Morning came with a mist from the river, which only later dissolved into the perpetual rain which had been falling for weeks now. It was only occasionally that the weather cleared sufficiently to afford a good view. During those bright intervals it was evident that their guide had done his work well. Looking across the arc of a wide bend in the river they could see the white houses of Santarem ranged along the quays of the town, and on the quays they could see a good deal of bustle and activity. Then on the farther bank they saw something which set Dodd's heart beating strangely—a line of red-coats; the watery sun was reflected from the sloped musket barrels. There was British infantry across the river, then—Dodd had seen Portuguese cavalry there a long time ago. The red streak moved steadily along the river bank down stream; as he watched a dip in the contour of land gradually swallowed it up. So that enough troops had been spared from the garrison of the Lines to establish a solid force beyond the river. The French were properly ringed in now, between the Lines and the irregulars and the river and troops across the river. But that still did not explain the cannonade at Santarem; they had to wait a little longer for the explanation of that.

Soon guns boomed from the farther bank, and were instantly answered by guns from Santarem. Dodd, gazing anxiously across the bend, tried to make out at what the British guns were aimed, but it was hard to detect the fall of shot at that distance. Then he saw something else. A long streak of smoke shot from the bank, and described a wide curve across the river, ending among the houses of Santarem. Another followed it, and another, while the fire of the French guns was redoubled.

Dodd scratched his head in some bewilderment before he hit on an explanation of the phenomenon. Rockets! There had long been one or two rocket batteries in the English army, the source of a good deal of amusement to everybody. Rockets were such unreliable and irregular weapons. They might serve to terrify savages, perhaps, or to—Dodd guessed their purpose now. There was something in Santarem which the English were anxious to set on fire. Presumably that something must be within sight of the farther bank, and therefore must be close to the water's edge. Dodd was enough of a soldier to guess what it must be— a bridge or bridging material, boats or pontoons and roadway stuff. Dodd pulled at the bristling beard which had sprouted on his chin during the last few weeks and fell into deep thought.

Rocket after rocket curved across the river, while the guns from Santarem strove to put the rocket battery out of action and the guns on the other bank strove to silence them. In the middle of the action they heard a noise overhead which startled them. They looked at each other in fear and cowered back amid the myrtles. There came a cracking of whips and a clattering of harness and loud orders in French from the field under whose edge they lay. Horses neighed and men shouted. Dodd knew what was happening, but he dared not make a sound to enlighten his companions, even if his command of the language had enabled him to do so. He knew the sound of a battery going into action well enough.

Bernardino and the stunted man did not have to wait long in ignorance. With an appalling crash the six guns fifty yards behind them opened simultaneously. They had been moved up here to take the English in flank. The powder smoke from the guns, keeping low along the ground, came drifting down upon them. It would have set them coughing had they dared to allow themselves to cough. They heard the orders of the officers correcting the direction and elevation, and then the guns roared out again, and again, and again. Dodd was too low down to see what they were firing at, and he certainly was not going to try and find out. They were in deadly peril here in their hiding-place. They crouched down among the myrtle bushes, striving after complete concealment. Bernardino's lips were moving in prayer, but he was stupid, because he allowed the noise to add to his terror; despite his common sense, he could not make himself believe that the appalling explosions added nothing to their danger.

A moment of far greater danger came, all

the same, a few minutes later, when someone came to the edge of the river some distance away and looked over the water. The three of them lay frozen among the bushes—a searching glance from the new arrival might have disclosed them nevertheless. But he was not looking for men; he would have been extremely surprised to find an English soldier and a couple of Portuguese hidden under the very muzzles of his guns. He was looking for a place to water the horses, and the immediate neighbourhood, with a ten-foot drop to the surface of the river, was clearly not suitable. It was at a place three hundred yards away that the horses were eventually led to the water's edge—dangerous enough, but not too much so.

Dodd and Bernardino and the stunted man cowered among the bushes all day long, while the guns roared above them at intervals whenever their target was not obscured, while the horses were being watered quite close at hand, and the rockets still strung their arcs of smoke across the river. As far as Dodd could see, they produced not the least effect. For a rocket to start a fire while a numerous and vigilant fire-fighting party was on the watch would call for a far more propitious combination of circumstances than could ever be expected: and, anyway, no rocket could be expected to come to earth less than a hundred yards from the point aimed at. In fact, in

Dodd's opinion, everyone concerned was simply wasting gunpowder.

Perhaps the British officer in command of the rocket battery and artillery beyond the river came to the same opinion as the day wore on, for the firing died away. The battery in the field above the trio ceased fire, presumably because the enemy had withdrawn from sight, and silence descended again, broken only by occasional bursts of laughter and conversation from the unseen artillery men, and by the unceasing gurgle of the eddies of the river below them.

Later in the afternoon their good fortune displayed itself once more. They heard the clink and clatter of harness as the horses were put to the guns again, and they heard the whip cracking and shouts of the drivers as the beasts were stimulated to the wild effort necessary to heave the guns out of the earth into which they had sunk under the impulse of their firing. Then the guns jingled and clattered across the field, and they heard the noise of their progress rise to a roar when they reached the paved high road, and the roar gradually died away with the increasing distance.

The battery had departed, and Bernardino, with the impatience of his years and inexperience, began to stretch his cramped limbs as a matter of course; he intended to climb up and look over the edge of the cliff to see if any of the enemy remained above them, but Dodd seized his shoulder and forced him into passivity again. Whether the enemy had gone or not they would not be able to move from their present position until nightfall. To look over the edge was running a risk for no reward save the satisfaction of curiosity, and although Dodd's curiosity in the matter was just as acute as Bernardino's he had no intention of imperilling himself on that account. No comfort of mind or body could compare in Dodd's opinion with the negative comfort of remaining alive as long as duty permitted—this opinion of Dodd's goes far to explain why he had been able to survive five campaigns.

They stayed for the rest of the day immobile among the bushes, wetted through at intervals by the rain. They would probably pay no immediate penalty for that; colds in the head are very infrequent among people living all their time out of doors. Yet they could boast no such immunity from pneumonia or rheumatic fever, and in after years, were they to live so long, they would be bent and crippled and agonized with rheumatism—say in thirty years' time. But men in the early twenties—least of all soldiers—do not often stop to think about possible illness in thirty years' time.

All Dodd's cogitation during the afternoon led him no nearer any definite decision. There was bridging material at Santarem which the

English wanted burnt; that made it his duty to burn it if he could. That was clear enough; it was none of Dodd's business to bear in mind the fact that the motive for desiring the destruction of the bridge might be very slight indeed—no stronger than the result of the very ordinary decision that it ought to be a good move to destroy anything that the enemy considers it desirable to construct. If horse, foot, and guns had been brought up to burn the bridge, then Dodd ought to try as well; the unanswerable question at the moment was how to do it.

He could see Santarem clearly enough, and the towering warehouses on the quays. There were several thousand men there; at night (such must be the crowding in the town) there would be men asleep or on guard all round the stuff, and upon it and underneath it. Reluctantly he decided that it would be an impossible task—as far as he could judge at the moment—to penetrate into Santarem and set fire to the bridge. It might be done by a man not in uniform, but to discard his uniform would make him a spy, liable to the death of a spy, and Dodd, with the usual fantastic notions of military honour, refused to consider it, although he knew well enough that if the French were to catch him this far within their cantonments they would probably shoot him or hang him anyway.

Yet, although the business seemed so

impossible, Dodd did not entirely put away all thought of it. Some other way round the difficulty might present itself. Prolonged reconnaissance from the inland corner of the wood where they had found their present guide might suggest something—Dodd could not imagine what, but he hoped. So as dusk crept down upon them he made ready with the others for a return to the stunted man's hiding-place.

In the twilight they allowed Bernardino to satisfy his earlier wish to climb up and look over the top of the little cliff: sure enough, the field beyond was deserted and the way to the main road was clear. When it was fully dark they started stiffly out upon the return journey, over the fields and along the ditches, past the village where, at this early hour in the evening, the fires blazed with their full volume, until not very much past midnight they reached the edge of the wood, and could warm themselves by a sharp walk to the hut where the old man had died.

They were all desperately tired and hungry and short-tempered. Dodd was disappointed at the unsatisfactory result of his investigations, but he was not half so annoyed as his companions. They had gone short of sleep for two nights, they had spent a day in unutterable discomfort and a great deal of terror, they were wet and muddy and cramped, solely because of his unreasonable wish to see

Santarem—that was how they expressed it to themselves. Even Bernardino's faith in Dodd was shaken for the moment. He had failed to produce any new ingenious scheme for the discomfiture of the French, and Bernardino was one of those who demand new things. He grumbled and complained as they crowded into the little hut seeking its not-completely-effective shelter from the rain. He objected violently when Dodd's knees and elbows dug into him in their cramped sleeping space. But he was too tired to keep it up. Soon they were all three of them fast asleep, packed together like pigs in a sty, and nearly as dirty. The rain dripped monotonously through the trees.

CHAPTER SIXTEEN

In the wet morning the usual three military problems of offence and defence and supply presented themselves. They shared the last of their bread with the stunted man—there was no knowing how he had been maintaining himself before they met him; badly enough presumably—and tried to discuss the next move. Bernardino, in fact, was so disgruntled by recent events that he presumed to press plans upon Dodd. He wanted to go back to the village, taking the stunted man with them as a fresh recruit, and resume the harassing of the battalion there. To Bernardino it was obviously the thing to do. On the hill there was food and there were friends and an enemy to attack. Here in the wood there seemed nothing. When Dodd said 'See Santarem' and persisted in saying it he grew exasperated. He knew nothing of strategy; he could not grasp the possibly supreme importance of the bridging materials at Santarem.

The stunted man contributed little to the discussion. If he had ever had any initiative— and there was no means of telling—it had all evaporated with the death of his father. He wanted to kill Frenchmen, but he seemed willing enough to do it under the direction of others. He said nothing when Dodd said 'See Santarem' in a tone of finality and rose and hitched his rifle on his shoulder and set off towards the far corner of the wood, although Bernardino stamped his feet with annoyance.

Bernardino followed Dodd, sulkily, in the end, and the stunted man came too, without a word. There was small satisfaction to be gained from the distant view of the land in front of Santarem. The little town was walled on this side, with gates, which would make it supremely difficult to achieve an unobserved entrance. Bernardino fidgeted with irritation while Dodd looked this way, and that way, and tried to ask the stunted man questions.

In the end coincidence brought about a dramatic change in Dodd's plans, and delighted Bernardino's heart. Across the half or three-quarters of a mile of flat land which lay between them and the town they suddenly saw signs of some important move outside the gate on the upstream end of the town. They saw a little column of troops march out. After them came a wagon—at that distance they could make out no details, but Dodd was sure it was a wagon and not a gun. There came another wagon, and another, and another, and another. Wagon followed wagon until Dodd was sure that he was not observing a minor military move—the transfer of a convoy, or something of that order. It became pressingly important to his mind to discover what this was.

'Go to road. See,' said Dodd.

He turned and hurried back into the wood, with Bernardino delightedly following him, for that must be the direction they must follow to return to the village.

They hurried through the wood at the best speed possible to them when they had to be on guard at every step lest some French patrol should be prowling near at hand. Even in the heart of the forest they could hear the sound of the wagon train on the *pavé*—a low rumble rising a note or two in the scale whenever a wagon crossed over a culvert or a bridge.

At last they reached a point in the wood whence they could look down on the high road, and Dodd threw himself on his face and edged forward to peer round a trunk of a tree. The others crouched near, and ever the rain poured down on them. The head of the column, with the vanguard of troops, had already passed, but what followed was far more interesting. Dodd had been right when he had suspected the French of bridge construction. The first vehicles were odd-shaped things, each composed of two artillery caissons linked together. On these were piled pontoons, huge, clumsy boats nested into each other, four or five together. Their number was great—section after section lumbered by. Dodd took note of the animals drawing them along—wretched, underfed horses with their ribs starting through their coats; it was a wonder that they could drag themselves along, to say nothing of the loads behind them. The French soldiers driving them displayed little care as to their condition, flogging the poor brutes along as they slipped and stumbled over the cobbles. Dodd readily decided that a few weeks more of this underfed life would leave the French army with no transport animals at all. To the pontoon-laden caissons succeeded, at length, service wagons and country carts heaped with all the miscellaneous accessories of military bridges; there were four carts laden with rope and quite thirty laden with timber.

But before the last caisson had gone by Dodd had resolved to do what he could to interfere with the march of the bridging train.

No one knew better than he, who had served in so many convoy guards, how helpless is a long train of wagons strung out along the road. And he knew, too, that to kill one of the enemy's horses was quite as helpful as killing one of the enemy's men. He looked round at his two followers.

'*Caballos*,' he said, '*Caballos*,' and pushed his rifle forward.

They took aim beside him, and the three shots rang out almost together. One horse in a team of six fell in its traces; another, plunging and kicking on three legs, made evident the fact that the fourth was broken. Instantly Dodd leaped to his feet and dashed back among the trees, with the others at his heels, to where he could reload undisturbed.

'Horses,' said Dodd again, as he rammed the bullet home.

The others nodded. They could understand this method of warfare. Dodd pelted through the wood parallel with the road for a short space before changing direction to the edge again. There was confusion in the convoy. The wagon at whose team they had fired was stationary and helpless, and everything behind it was pulling up. Drivers were seeking their weapons, men were shouting, horses were plunging—there was all the confusion of a sudden surprise attack. The escort parties at the head and rear of the column were each of them half a mile away or more; the three were safe for some time from any counter-attack, for the drivers had, as was only to be expected, an exaggerated idea of the force attacking them, and were hampered by the necessity of looking after their teams. A young officer came galloping up the road to the place of the jam. For the moment Dodd pointed his rifle at him, but he refrained from pulling the trigger when he guessed what order the officer was going to give. He glowered round at his companions to enforce on them the same self-restraint. At the officer's order the wagon behind the one which was stationary pulled out of the line and began to go up past the point of stoppage; the rest of the long line made preparations to follow. Just when the overtaking wagon was diagonally across the road Dodd fired again, and next second the jam was complete; two helpless wagons completely blocked the narrow paved road. Drivers raved and horses kicked while Dodd reloaded with all the speed five years of practice could give. A third volley brought down more horses still and perfected the work. After that for several hectic minutes each of the three loaded and fired at will, bringing down a horse here and a horse there, until Dodd made his companions cease fire. He had to shake them by the shoulders to compel their attention, so excited had they grown. Some of the drivers had found their muskets and were blazing back at random into the wood; bullets were rapping sharply on trees here and there, but that was not the reason for Dodd's cessation of fire. There was a body of troops hurrying back from the head of the column; another hurrying up from the tail. They were still some distance off when Dodd ran away, intent on living to fight another day. As they ran breathlessly through the wood, Dodd found himself regretting that he had not thirty men with him instead of two; there would be a fine game open to them then in the attack on this long, vulnerable column. Three was too small a force altogether.

When the escort reached the point in the road whence the firing had come they halted for a moment at a loss, for there was no firing now. In the end they plunged into the wood, but only for a short distance. They could find no trace of the enemy, and as they plunged about in the undergrowth the officers were uneasily conscious that meanwhile they were leaving the line of wagons unguarded—an uneasiness which was greatly accentuated immediately after-wards by the sound of firing from high up towards the head of the column. It was a lively day for the convoy escort as well as for the drivers. The escort spent their time running up and down a couple of miles of road in hopeless dashes after an enemy which fled at their earliest approach and yet was always ready to reappear elsewhere and resume their harassing attacks. If the three hundred men of the escort had been strung along the road trying to guard every point they would have been just as useless—one man to every ten yards. Meanwhile the drivers were engaged in cutting out injured horses, in replacing them with animals from the few teams which could spare them, and getting the wagons along somehow.

In the end, the situation was relieved by the arrival of reinforcements. A battalion—the fourth of the Forty-Sixth—was called out of its billets in a village some distance up the road, and another came up from Santarem, which the convoy had just left. Then they were able to post guards in sufficient strength along the dangerous lengths of road, and even to spare men to manhandle teamless wagons out of the way. Yet all this took time; by the end of the day the wagon train had progressed exactly three miles.

Dodd, crouching with his two companions at the far end of the wood, whither they had been driven by the new arrivals, could feel pleased with his day's work, despite the fact that they were all three of them so exhausted that they could hardly stand. He had regained his old ascendancy too. Bernardino was enormously amused by what they had done; despite his fatigue he still broke into little chuckles at the recollection of the exasperated wagon drivers and the jams and confusion of the train and the harassed running about of the escort. It had taken a thousand men in the end to guard those wagons against three enemies.

It is to be feared that Dodd enjoyed undue credit on this account—both Bernardino and the stunted man believed (and the difficulties of language prevented a clearing up of the situation) that this attack on the convoy had been planned from the first, and that the dangerous visit to inspect Santarem, which they had condemned so bitterly earlier, was a necessary part of the scheme. It sent up Dodd's stock with a bound. Several times Bernardino told Dodd, who did not understand what he said, and the stunted man, who did not appear specially interested, all about what they had done that day.

Even Bernardino's excitement died away in time, and allowed him to meditate upon the matter which was now occupying all Dodd's attention—the matter of their hunger and the absence of means to satisfy it. Bernardino's ebullition of spirits changed to peevishness, when suddenly the stunted man rose and walked away through the darkness under the trees. Bernardino was actually too tired and hungry to ask where he was going. Dodd pulled in his belt and tried to reconcile himself to an evening without supper and the prospect of a morrow without breakfast. He had actually sunk into a fitful doze when they heard the stunted man, seeking them, call to them in a guarded tone. They replied, and he appeared, a shadowy shape, through the trees. He pressed something wet and faintly warm into Dodd's hands, and presumably made a similar present to Bernardino.

'What is this?' asked Bernardino.

'Horse,' said the stunted man, who was a man of few words.

For once one of Dodd's subordinates had been cleverer than he—Dodd had forgotten all about the dozen dead horses along the edge of the main road, but the stunted man had remembered them, and had found his way to one. Not merely that, but he had used his wits well when he had reached his objective. Even in the dark and in the imminent danger of being surprised by a stray enemy he had remembered that it would be far too dangerous to light a fire for cooking with so many of the enemy near, and he had realized that a lump of muscle hacked from a starving horse might well defy their teeth were it uncooked. So he had ripped open the horse's belly and had plunged into its still warm entrails in search of its liver, from which he had cut the generous portions which they were now considering.

Dodd had eaten horse before—no soldier could serve five campaigns in the Peninsula, where small armies are beaten and large armies starve, without doing so—but always before it had at least made a pretence at being cooked. But he had never been as hungry before as he was now, and it was too dark to see what he was eating and, anyway, he had led the life of a savage for two months. He took a tentative nibble at his lump, and followed it with another, and yet another.

Before very long he had made a good meal in the darkness and so had the others. And the fact that they had all been living lives of hard physical exertion in the fresh air for so long blessed them with digestions which could even master uncooked cart horse.

After that they all slept well and deeply until Dodd woke and roused his companions— he had the knack of being able to wake at any hour he decided upon before going to sleep. It was two hours before dawn and they were stupid and weary, but they followed Dodd when he began to make his way back through the wood to the high road. They crossed the road safely, for it was still dark, and went up into the hill opposite, and then it dawned upon Bernardino what was in Dodd's mind, and he clapped his fist into his hand with delight. For by the end of yesterday the convoy had progressed beyond the point where the forest bordered the road; any further attack upon it would have to be made from the hill this other side, the hill whence weeks ago they had harassed the dragoons, and fought their first skirmish with the Forty-Sixth.

But there is nothing so fragile as a military

plan. When dawn revealed the convoy breaking up its ordered ranks from its camp in the fields at the roadside beyond the wood, they could see that the reinforcements for the convoy escort which had arrived yesterday evening had stayed with it and were prepared to march with it today. Instead of having merely a hundred and fifty men both at the head and at the tail of the column, a mile and a half apart, there were now detachments of very considerable strength all the way along. Dodd looked down at the column from the crest of the hill, and decided not to interfere with it. Long service under a general who never lost a gun in action had taught even the men in the ranks of his army the distinction between bold enterprises and foolhardy ones. Neither of Dodd's followers questioned his decision: their faith in him was profound.

They dragged their weary limbs along after him as he walked along the hill-top towards the village. Perhaps Bernardino experienced a feeling of pleasurable anticipation at the prospect of returning to Agostina's embraces; perhaps he was too tired.

The nearer they came to the village the more cautious were their movements, until at last they reached the point where they could look down the slope to where the village nestled between the two hills. Everything seemed much as usual. There were only a few French to be seen moving among the houses—

Dodd guessed that it was from here that most of the reinforcements for the convoy escort had been drawn. There were a few engaged on their eternal hunt for something edible, for nettles at least if not for hidden stores of food, and a few sick and wounded limping about here and there. Across the deep valley, on the slopes of the other, steeper hill, they could see nothing at all of importance, but that was only to be expected. It was not the custom of the outlaws to expose themselves.

Dodd changed their direction away from the river over towards the stony lane, which they crossed with all due precaution, just as Dodd and Bernardino had crossed it in the opposite direction five days before. Now they were very near to their friends. Dodd felt quite pleased at the prospect of seeing them again. He increased his pace as he scrambled up the steep paths, as much as the steepness would allow, and the necessity for taking care not to run into either a French patrol or a Portuguese sentry too ready to fire.

They found no sentry at the summit of the path, even though Dodd had purposefully chosen a path which led towards a point where a sentry ought to have been found. Dodd clicked his tongue with annoyance as he halted there for breath; the sentry's absence seemed to indicate slackness on the part of the garrison unless some important duty had called him elsewhere. Even if they were certain that the greater part of the enemy was away on the high road they should still keep their watch unbroken. Dodd looked round, but the hillside was far too irregular and overgrown for him to see far. He pushed on over the brow of the hill, down the dip, and up the next slope.

And then both he and Bernardino caught sight of something which made them halt abruptly where they stood, and look, and look again, not understanding what they saw. There was a little level stretch of ground here, where the rocks were more naked than usual, and the bushes lower, but at the farther side of it a thorn tree maintained a precarious existence. The branches of the thorn tree grew downwards a little, so as partly to screen whatever was underneath them. Through this screen they could faintly see two men leaning against the trunk in attitudes of strange abandon. One was bent oddly forward with his arms hanging queerly limp, the other was lolling back in a manner which made it appear strange that he did not slip down to the ground.

It was all very mysterious and eerie. Dodd cocked his rifle as he picked his way over the rocks towards the tree. It was not until he was close to it that he could see the details. The two men had been nailed to the tree with bayonets—their own, presumably, as their scabbards were empty—although it was apparent that whoever was responsible had

164

been merciful enough to shoot them afterwards. Dodd looked at the dead faces. He knew them, despite the distortion of the features. They were two Portuguese, two of the men who had helped him defend the hill. One of them was Pedro who had cut the wounded Frenchman's throat after the ambushing.

Bernardino at Dodd's elbow was pouring forth prayers and oaths intermingled. The stunted man, as ever, said nothing. To him this was only two more corpses in a land where death took his hundreds daily. Dodd, in the end, forced himself to take the same view of it, although the sight had strangely unnerved him and left him pale under his tan. He turned away and resumed his journey over the hill. Bit by bit the whole tragedy revealed itself. The hill had been stormed during their absence. Another dead man, one of the garrison, lay in the path down to the river. Old Maria lay dead at the mouth of the cave beyond the secret ford. It was possible to guess a little of what had happened to her before she died.

But it was not possible for Dodd to guess all the details. He could not guess, and he never would know, that the colonel of the battalion in the village had at last brought himself to confess his own weakness, and had borrowed the services of two battalions of Ney's Sixth Corps to aid him clear the mountain of the brigands who plagued him there. Dodd never knew of the onslaught of these terrible men who had marched by night to launch a surprise at dawn. He never knew, fortunately perhaps, of the torture which was applied to one of the captives to make him reveal the secret of the ford, nor of what the brutes did to Agostina and the little girls.

But it became clear enough in the course of the day that the mountain was deserted and empty. The men and the boys were dead. The women—save old Maria—and the girls were missing. Thirteen hundred men, attacking concentrically from all round, had swept the place bare, and left no living thing upon it. Nor could Ney's men be really blamed for what they had done to their prisoners. They had carried on a nightmare war in Spain and Portugal for three endless years now. Often had they seen what the enemy did to their friends. The men they had captured had been taken with arms in their hands and without uniforms, and so deserved to die. The women were as bad as the men, and anyway soldiers needed relaxation during three years' campaigning. And if the poor fools had only sense enough to submit to the all powerful emperor the women would not be interfered with quite so violently.

All food, of course, had been taken away. Dodd found consolation in the thought that what would make thirty days' food for twenty people would only make one day's food for five hundred, and actually, although he did not know it, thirteen hundred men had shared it—barely more than a mouthful apiece.

To Dodd and Bernardino the hill seemed accursed. They remembered the jolly people with whom they had lived there so long, people who had faced death at their sides over and over again. Dodd was too serious-minded a man to be able to smile—as many soldiers would—over the fact of the mere coincidence that he should have decided at that moment to go and see why the guns were firing at Santarem should have preserved his life when the others died.

Dodd would allow nothing to be done, all the same, to alter the things on the hill. The two dead men remained nailed to their tree to rot, Maria still lay in her dreadful attitude at the mouth of the cave. There was too much chance that anything he might do in the matter would disclose to any fresh exploring party from the village that there were still some survivors on the hill.

CHAPTER SEVENTEEN

Sergeant Godinot came to find that, despite the desperately hard work demanded of him and his men, life in Santarem was far more to his liking than life with the battalion in the village. The very work was a blessing; they were at least doing something instead of rotting in their billets while the eternal rain drummed on the roofs, and the hard-bitten veterans of the Second and Sixth Corps were far better working partners than the helpless disease-ridden recruits of his own battalion— except for Dubois, of course, who was his boyhood's friend. They got the town mill working soon, and the town ovens, so that the men could have bread to eat instead of the pestilent corn porridge. With the lightheartedness of the best type of French soldier they soon organized among themselves a town band which gave concerts whenever work permitted. The officers walked about the streets with women on their arms, which made the place very homely, even though some of the women wore men's uniforms and none of them as they flaunted through the town could possibly be mistaken for other than what they were.

There were other women in the town, too, women who avoided men's eyes and slunk along by the walls, women who wept and women who sometimes killed themselves, women whom Ney's godless veterans of the Sixth Corps had caught in their foraging expeditions inland.

The bridge made rapid progress towards completion, thanks to old General Éblé. He was everywhere at once, urging and commanding and inspecting. There was always a flurry and a speeding up whenever he appeared, whether it was in the forges where men laboured to make steel saws and adzes out of wrought-iron balcony rails, or in the nail recovery workshop where men laboriously straightened and repointed nails, or in the row of houses which men were feverishly pulling down for the sake of their timber, or in the paint works, or in the boat-building shed where Godinot spent most of his time, or in the rope works where men were trying to perform miracles.

Perhaps the most popular employment was the housebreaking—literally housebreaking—because the old houses which were being pulled down were infested with rats which could often be caught in the course of the work. A roasted rat made a splendid addition to one's daily ration during the frequent weeks when no meat was issued. Men who had been lucky in the matter of loot earlier in the campaign were known to pay as much as a silver dollar for a fat rat, although it was hard to find sellers here where there was nothing for money to buy and no apparent prospect of ever reaching home.

That was the worst part of the life, even worse than the food. No one knew what was happening outside the ranks of the army in which they were serving. The emperor in whose name they were fighting might be dead, the Russians might be in Paris, or the other armies in Spain might have been pushed back to the Pyrenees leaving them isolated here in Portugal. They knew nothing whatever save that they were holding a patch of country twenty miles square from which they would have to wring their food until something—no one knew what—should happen. The building of the bridge was an anodyne for despair, but not a satisfactory one. Old soldiers could not picture the army crossing the river by perilous pontoon bridges while an active and vigilant enemy was ready to fall upon them in the act of passing. And if they should pass, there only lay on the other side of the river the barren plains of southern Portugal. And if they stayed, they starved. And the only retreat open to them was over the awful mountain roads by which they had come, which was a prospect just as appalling as the other two. The dreadful feeling of helpless isolation demoralized everyone.

There were bitter jests made in the workshops about Godinot's uncle—Dubois had told the others of the relationship. The only route by which a new factor could enter into the situation was from the south, where, two hundred miles away beyond the Tagus, Soult with General Godinot's aid was holding down Andalusia. If he should abandon his principality and march to the Tagus something fresh might happen; most of the men believed that it was in consequence of this possibility that the bridge was being constructed. Every day some jester would ask Godinot if there were any news from his uncle, and when they would have the pleasure of meeting him. In fact, the bridge was alluded to by most of the men as Godinot's uncle's bridge. But Godinot's uncle never came, however often they asked about him.

The construction of the pontoons progressed, nevertheless, in the face of difficulties and discouragement. It was heartbreaking work. Everything had to be botched and makeshift. The knees and ribs of the boats which ought to have grown naturally to shape had to be hacked out of floor-joists with badly-tempered saws and axes, which bent like lead when they were incautiously used. Bending the rotten timber into shape for the strakes was a tedious business, which had to be repeated over and over again before a result remotely satisfactory was attained. Nails were truly and literally more precious than gold; they had to be employed with niggling economy and every one had to be accounted for. The gaping seams left open by unavoidable bad workmanship had to be caulked with any odd materials that came to hand. Yet the caulking must be perfect, for when an army of a hundred thousand men with guns and wagons is pouring over a bridge there must be no delay to bail out pontoons.

The paint which the experimenters produced was almost useless—when daubed on wood and immersed in water as a test most of it floated up to the surface in an hour or two. The experimental cordage stretched and snapped and disintegrated. The one problem which was solved to the satisfaction of everyone was that of the anchors—in Portugal there could not be any difficulty in finding a sufficiency of big rocks for that purpose.

As soon as each pontoon—great, lumbering, over-heavy things that they were—was completed, it was brought down to the quay and launched into the river by the slipway Godinot helped to build. Here it swung to moorings while being tested for staunchness and stability; quite two out of three of them demanded further attention before they could be passed as fit to bear a roadway to carry an army. Then they were hauled out and stacked on the quays, alongside the growing mass of roadway material and cables.

The river ran torrentially; it boiled along the quay, and in the prevailing westerly winds its surface was whipped, by the action of the wind against the current, into big, lumpy waves crested with foam. Godinot used to look out across the mass of mad water with gloomy forebodings. A bridge laid across it would bank up the current against itself. If one cable were to break, one anchor to drag, he could picture the whole bridge breaking into

172

fragments and being swept downstream, leaving the army if it were crossing at the time divided into two helpless halves.

Godinot saw more than that when he looked across the river. Already the presence of Portuguese cavalry had been noted on the low, featureless opposite bank. One morning Godinot caught Dubois' arm and pointed. There was a red stripe showing against the neutral grey-green, a stripe which moved steadily across the landscape, up and down the slight undulations, and along its upper edge the stripe was bordered with a rim of flashing steel. There was a brigade of red-coats marching there.

'Englishmen!' said Dubois, staring, while Godinot turned hastily away to report his discovery to the nearest officer.

When he came back he found Dubois still standing on the quay, staring with parted lips at the next development. There were half a dozen little things like caterpillars on the opposite bank now, and as Godinot reached Dubois' side they all swung round and broke into halves, and there was infinite bustle among the little dots above water's edge. Then a white puff like a ball of cotton-wool appeared for a second, a sudden fountain of water from the surface of the river just in front of them, and a cannon-ball, ricochetting, sang over their heads like a hive of bees and then crashed into the upper storey of the warehouse behind them. Another immediately afterwards hit the edge of the quay some distance away and caused such a spray of flying chips of stone that it was a miracle no one was hurt.

'It appears to me,' said Dubois, aping the imperturbability of a veteran, 'as if the English have begun to take notice of our activities here.'

Then the next cannon-ball splintered a door dose at hand and Dubois dropped his nonchalance and ran to cover behind the warehouse as fast as Godinot did.

For the moment all work ceased in Santarem. Mounted messengers clattered through the streets and dashed out of the gates to bring batteries into action to drive away these insolent interrupters, while cannon-balls came crashing into the town at regular intervals. Then a shell exploded with a sharp crack overhead, and sprayed shrapnel bullets over the exact centre of the main street, causing several casualties among the crowd gathered there. That caused annoyance to supersede interest. The British artillery was the only one to employ this new missile, and it was universally disliked and dreaded by the French.

However, the shells that came over were few, because the enemy had come to destroy bridging material and workshops, not men. Godinot, peering round the corner of the warehouse, saw a moored pontoon fly suddenly into fragments when a round-shot hit it fair and true in the middle. There were gaping holes now here and there in the solid walls of the warehouses. A sudden enormous clatter of hoofs announced the arrival of someone specially important; so it was—no less a person than Marshal Masséna himself, the general commanding in chief, with General Éblé and Marshal Ney and a couple of score of aides-de-camp and his renegade Portuguese advisers and three dozen mounted orderlies.

Masséna climbed down from his horse and hobbled stiffly down a side alley to the river. He grabbed Dubois by the arm and made him stand out beyond the corner of the warehouse so that he could rest his ponderous telescope on his shoulder. Godinot watching the expression on Dubois' face could not help but be amused. There was doubtless honour in supporting the telescope of a Prince of the Empire, but it was an honour Dubois could have well done without when it involved standing clear of all cover while a bombardment was going on.

Masséna gave back his telescope to his aide-de-camp and turned away without a word, and Dubois scuttled gratefully back to Godinot behind the warehouse. It was not long before guns came clashing and clattering into the town and took up position in the alleyways leading to the river and opened fire on the enemy. Downstream they heard other guns take up the chorus. Whoever the British general was across the water, his hopes must far have outrun his judgement if he expected to destroy the French bridges with a single six-pounder horse battery. Soon thirty guns were firing in reply, with all the advantages of concealment and cover. The British battery stood up to a good deal of heavy punishment, but it was more than flesh and blood could stand in the end, and they limbered up and went away.

Then the French officers were able to collect their workmen at last and begin the day's work. Not much damage had been done. A single pontoon had been sunk and the workshops had been a little knocked about; that was all. Later in the day the British horse artillery tried new tactics, galloping up suddenly to an unexpected position and putting in a few hasty shots which came crashing into the houses, but each time they were driven off speedily by the counter-batteries awaiting them. Not even the British artillery, with its brilliant officers, and magnificent material, had yet devised a method of firing the guns from a concealed position while a forward observation officer controlled the aim.

Yet the British were not easily deterred from an objective on which they had set their hearts. Next morning revealed to the French a series of low mounds on the opposite bank; the British had started to throw up earthworks for gun emplacements there, and not all the fire of the French guns during the day could knock them to pieces.

And the morning after that the earthworks were completed. The guns were mounted there, and only their muzzles, peeping through the embrasures, could be seen from the French bank, while the men were afforded almost complete protection. There were other instruments of destruction besides guns too. With a hiss and a scream a long trail of smoke shot up from the earthworks and came curving over to the quays, falling with a splutter of blue fire beside a warehouse. Fortunately, perhaps, there were very few occasions when the rockets made as good a shot as that. The workmen, Dubois and Godinot among them, were paraded under cover with buckets and barrels of water ready to fight fires, but their services were hardly called upon. Some of the rockets dived straight into the river; others curved away in the wind and fell absurd distances away. One or two even soared into the air and fell back on the English side.

Yet despite all this bad practice, and despite the fact that French artillery was sent far out to right and to left in an endeavour to enfilade the English earthworks, Godinot knew that this English demonstration would be effective

177

enough in one respect. There were enough roundshot coming into the town to make work in the workshops risky, but a more important consideration was that the operation of casting bridges over the river at Santarem (if ever it were contemplated) would now be so difficult as almost to be impossible, now that there was artillery in solid works to oppose the passage. When, late in the afternoon, carts and wagons and artillery caissons—as much transport as the whole army could boast, Godinot guessed—began to stream into the town his suspicions were confirmed.

'We shall move tomorrow,' he said to Dubois, nodding at the wagons parking in the main street.

'How do you know?' asked Dubois, the ever sceptical. 'There are lots of reasons why—'

'Mark my words,' said Godinot, 'we shall move tomorrow, if we don't move tonight.'

He was quite right. In the evening all the bridge builders were hard at work loading their nearly completed bridges on the wagons. It was an immense task, for the amount of material they had put together was colossal. The only means that could be devised of transporting the pontoons themselves was by tying the artillery caissons together in pairs and balancing the big, clumsy boats on top. For the actual hoisting of them up, the blocks and tackle once used for lifting wool bales, hanging outside the upper windows of the wool warehouses, came in exceedingly handy, and it was in devising ways and means of bringing these God-sent appliances into use that Godinot earned a word of praise from General Éblé. The cordage and, above all, the roadway timber occupied an immense number of wagons. Everyone was tired out and wet through—for of course the rain which had fallen at intervals during the day settled into a steady downpour at nightfall—by the time the loading was finished. Yet the order was given for the bridging party to be on parade at five o'clock in the morning—only three hours hence.

Even getting the immense convoy under way when morning came was a huge business. The emaciated horses slipped and fell on the cobbles, traces broke, lashings broke. But it was done at last. Carefully closed up, in obedience to the strict orders given, the convoy, a solid mile and a half of vehicles, began its slow course out of the town, in an up-stream direction, towards, as Dubois was actually able to work out for himself, the village where the fourth battalion of the Forty-Sixth was billeted. He and Godinot were marching with half the bridging party at the head of the column. Everyone was tired and sick and hungry and exceedingly bad-tempered, and no one, save, presumably, the officers, knew whither they were going.

The pace was funereal. Every few minutes

they had to halt in the rain to allow the dragging column to catch up with them, and every minute they grew wetter and at every halt they grew colder. Godinot, struggling and slipping on the *pavé,* was glad that he still possessed a good pair of boots. Boots were growing scarce in the French army; half the men round him, especially those detached from the Sixth Corps, had none at all. Their feet were, instead, tied up in bags of raw-hide obtained from the carcasses of the ration animals or from dead horses. They were comfortable from one point of view, in that worn with the hair inside they kept the feet warm, but in every other respect they were horribly unsuitable, and they were liable to wear out suddenly and leave their wretched possessor to tramp barefoot on the stony roads. Most of the men, too, were in rags barely sufficient for decency; a few had civilian clothes, coats or breeches, some of them significantly marked with bloodstains. Altogether they looked more like a mob of beggars than the bridging section of a regular army—dispirited beggars, moreover. The obvious check to the army's plans at Santarem had taken the heart out of them.

So that when, almost as soon as the convoy had started, there came the sound of distant musketry far down the column, everyone cursed and grumbled. A message from the rear halted the head of the column, and turned the

180

escort about on a hurried dash back to the focus of the trouble. Executed at the double, it was a long run for men underfed and overworked. When they arrived there was not a glimpse of the enemy, which was just what they expected. There were traces of their handiwork, all the same—wagons with half their horses dead, jammed across the road, wounded horses plunging and kicking, drivers trying to control their teams, officers swearing. The road here was bordered by a thick forest, in which, as the cursing escort realized, there was no chance at all of catching their elusive enemies. Moreover, hardly had they halted, panting, at the edge of the wood, than other shots were fired back towards whence they came, and half of them, the unfortunate Godinot and Dubois among them, had to run back again, only to find just another crippled team there to add to the difficulty of getting the convoy along.

As the blaspheming soldiers said, a guard of three hundred men ought to have been sufficient for a wagon column moving in the middle of the cantonments of an army of a hundred thousand, but in the Peninsula ordinary military axioms did not apply. In that broken and difficult country three hundred men could not guard a convoy a mile and a half long against an active enemy, and it was only too obvious that the enemy was still active here in the heart of the French territory.

Exactly how many of the enemy there were attacking the column no one really stopped to consider. Everyone took it for granted that not less than fifty at least would have the boldness to pester a large force in this way, which complicated enormously the question of breaking the escort up into detachments, or pursuing the enemy into the forest. And when the road set itself to the task of climbing over the spur of mountain which here ran down to the Tagus from the backbone of the Lisbon peninsula matters grew more difficult still, because now 'tracing' had to be resorted to— taking the team from one wagon to reinforce that of another to climb part way up the hill before descending to pick up the one left horseless. This naturally made for a long break in the column, and at either end of the break a muddle of stationary vehicles, with horses being taken out or put in, and everybody busy and distracted—an ideal mark for anyone who cared to take a long shot into the thick of it from the shelter of the forest.

A subtle difference in the quality of the sound of some of the shots fired caught Godinot's ear. There was a peculiar ring about them; they were the sounds of a rifle and not of a musket. He had heard that noise before, often enough. And listening carefully, he was sure only one rifle was firing. Then he guessed who was responsible—it was only natural, for it was just in this locality that his battalion had first fought the irregulars whom the green English rifleman had led. It confirmed Godinot in his notion that there must be a large party attacking them, for the green Englishman had been at the head of a considerable band at their last encounter. If Godinot and his companions had only known that the pests who were worrying them numbered only three in all they would have been considerably astonished, but they would not discover it if Dodd could help it. Dodd had learned his trade under a soldier with an acute ability to estimate relative values—the last man in the world to abandon a strategical position in order to score a tactical point.

So Sergeant Godinot did not know what to make of things when, at the end of a terribly exhausting day, he was chatting with Adjutant Doguereau of his battalion, which had been brought down from its billets to help bring the column through. Adjutant Doguereau gave Godinot the latest battalion gossip, and told Godinot of how they had just cleared—with the help of a couple of battalions from the Sixth Corps—the hill above the village of the gang who had plagued them.

'We wiped them out,' said Adjutant Doguereau. 'Every blessed one of them. The ones we caught we shot—you fellows of the bridging gang haven't left us with enough rope even to hang a brigand when we catch one. And the others we chased all over the hill and

183

got them all. One tried to swim the river. Poor devil! And the women! Oh, sonny, the women!'

Adjutant Doguereau smacked his lips, as he recalled that part of the affair, before he went on to tell Godinot the interesting story about the cave and the secret ford which led to it. Somehow Sergeant Godinot could not take much interest in that part of the story which told of how Ney's men had caught a child—a little boy—who had refused to disclose the secret even when threatened with death, but who had given it up readily enough when suitable methods were employed upon him.

'But what about the green Englishman?' asked Godinot.

'To hell with you and your green Englishman!' said Adjutant Doguereau. 'Half the battalion is still talking about a green Englishman. There never was one. I never saw him. Nor did anyone else that day.'

'You didn't catch one on the hill then?'

'No. There wasn't one, I say. There never was one.'

'Oh,' said Godinot, 'he's back in that forest there now.'

'How do you know? Have you seen him?'

'No,' said Godinot, 'but I heard him. I know a rifle shot when I hear one.'

'Bah!' replied Doguereau. 'And I know imagination when I hear it too.'

That sort of argument went no way towards

convincing hard-headed Sergeant Godinot.

The matter was so much on his nerves that it was a very decided relief next day that the column was not harassed in its march by a human enemy. Although the road had left the forest behind, the opposite side of it was flanked by the twin hills, the long, lower one and the short, steep one, between which lay the headquarters of the Forty-Sixth, and which constituted an ideal base for an attack by a force of any size on the lumbering convoy, even though the latter was now guarded by over a thousand men. Yet not a shot was fired all day; Godinot formed the opinion that the Englishman's force must indeed have been greatly diminished by the successful assault on the mountain which Doguereau had described. The fact that the Englishman himself had escaped tended to strengthen the suspicion which even the matter-of-fact Godinot had begun uneasily to cherish, to the effect that the Englishman must have some kind of supernatural power.

Godinot, however, did not have much time to think about it on that day. He was kept far too busy in the work of the convoy, for the steep descent on the other side of the spur proved to be more troublesome even than the ascent of the previous day. The rain still beat down relentlessly, and the road was full of potholes in which the overworked horses slipped and stumbled and broke their legs. Wagons fell over into ditches, and wagons out of control crashed into the ones ahead: a culvert, weakened by the rain, gave way under the weight passing over it and held up the whole line until the labouring bridging party had botched up some kind of new roadbed, across which doubled teams and a manhandling party a hundred strong could haul the stubborn wagons. Nightfall still found them short of their destination, and compelled to bivouac wretchedly by the roadside in the rain, on half-rations—and half-rations in this army meant quarter-rations. Nor was anybody's temper improved by the rumour which ran rapidly round the ranks next morning to the effect that a sentry had been found with his throat cut.

That afternoon, however, found them at the point to which they had been directed. It was a wild corner of Portugal. There was a little stone village here—Punhete it was called, Godinot understood, but clearly it was not on account of the village that the bridging train had been sent here. It was because of the river, the Zezere was its fantastic name, which came boiling down here from the mountains to lose itself in the broad waters of the Tagus. The bridging train established itself here, half a mile from the confluence, where the English artillery on the other side of the Tagus could not annoy it, and where it was out of observation. The portion of the bridges which had been completed was to be stacked here, and sheds were to be built to protect it from the weather, and launching slips for the boats were to be set up on the bank while the bridges were being completed. The theory was that here the pontoons could be launched, and even large sections of the bridge coupled together, before being floated down to the main river to take the English by surprise as soon as the passage of the Tagus was decided upon.

Sergeant Godinot looked at the racing mountain stream, and the rocks, and the eddies, and shook his head when he considered this plan. He knew something about the handling of boats on swift rivers, having spent many happy boyhood hours among the shoals of the Loire, and he could picture the muddle the unhandy landsmen of the bridging train would make of the affair. In his opinion it was just as well that sufficient material for two bridges was being constructed; when the attempt was to be made there might be just enough preserved from shipwreck and from being swept away downstream to make one bridge.

Godinot began to suspect that the building of the bridges was merely a gesture, something exactly comparable with the blind lunges of a strangling man—indeed the comparison between a strangling man and the French army in Portugal is a very apt one. The French felt themselves dying slowly, and were expending their energies in ill-directed efforts. Yet if no use were to be made of the bridges it would imply that soon they would have to retreat, and beyond the Zezere Godinot could see the mountains of central Portugal, rising up in peak after peak to mark the difficulties of the road over which they would have to go.

Yet the work had to be taken in hand all the same. The men were set to the colossal task of levelling an area beside the Zezere, and building sheds, and completing the bridges with materials taken from the village of Punhete. The men themselves had no billets this time; they had to construct little brushwood huts for themselves—as the veterans of the Second and Sixth Corps had long ago learnt how to do—in which they dragged out a miserable existence in the continual rain while they lived upon insufficient and irregular convoys of food sent up by a reluctant headquarters. As Dubois dolefully pointed out to Godinot, they had chosen the wrong job. When food is short the men who have the obtaining of it will see that they have enough before passing on any surplus to those who have none.

CHAPTER EIGHTEEN

The three vagabonds out on the hill were faced with the usual pressing military problem of supply. They were as ever horribly hungry, and they did not know where food was to come from. It is true that they had breakfasted in the morning off what was left of the horse's liver which the stunted man had gained for them the night before, but there had not been much, and what there was had been eaten twelve hours ago. Now it was growing dark and cold, and the world seemed a gloomy place.

Dodd could pull in his belt and philosophically endure the pangs of hunger, but Bernardino had not the temperament for that. Besides, Dodd was worried about the future. He could see no likely chance of gaining more food. What they could do was more than he could guess. Slow starvation up here on the hill was probably as pleasant a death as the French would provide for them if they were to go down and surrender. And even if he were assured of good treatment the prospect of surrendering was very nearly as hateful to him as death. He wanted to live. He wanted to rejoin his regiment. He wanted to find out what was the destination of the bridging train, and to do something towards destroying it.

This last desire marked a slight but significant change in Dodd's mental outlook which had been accomplished by the experiences of these last few weeks of independent action. Before that, even though he was a light infantryman and accustomed to some extent to acting by himself, he had been thoroughly imbued with the army tradition of looking for orders and doing nothing more than those orders dictated. That was all a private soldier was expected to do; indeed, to go beyond that usually meant trouble. Even in those days the usual retort of a non-commissioned officer was 'You thought? You're not paid to think. You're paid to obey orders'—a speech which has endured word for word even down to our day.

The rifle regiment tradition had never been as rigid as that of the line regiment, for in action the rifleman had more to do than merely to keep in step and in line with a thousand of his fellows whatever happened, but it was firm enough for any variation from it to mark out Rifleman Dodd as a man of some originality; five campaigns had already shown him to be a man of brute courage and resolution. It was a far cry from the skirmishing line at Busaco, farther still from the barrack square and the parade ground, and even farther from the bird-scaring and sheaf-binding and haymaking at the foot of the rolling Sussex Downs where he had spent his boyhood, to trying to play a part in the plans of Marshal the Prince of Essling and Lieut.-General Viscount Wellington, K.B.

Yet highfalutin plans would not fill Dodd's belly, and were no use at all to the hungry Bernardino. It was a very depressed and discontented Portuguese who resigned himself at last to a supperless bed amid the rocks at the side of Dodd. All the same, there was a ray of hope, because the stunted man, who never seemed to want to sleep, had gone out when they settled down, clearly—although he did not waste words on explaining his motives—to see what he could find to eat. Yesterday he had brought back a fine lump of horse's liver. Bernardino pinned his faith on the effort of the stunted man, and such was his hope that he actually went to sleep, hungry though he was.

Some hours after midnight, when just the faintest suspicion of greyness was come to relieve the blackness of night, Dodd awoke with a start. His ear had caught some strange noise, some noise which was not a natural one, and his subconscious mind had sifted it out from the other noises, and considered it, and finally had passed it on to his active mind and had wakened it instantly. Dodd sat up with his rifle in his hand; beside him Bernardino stirred and came to a slower awakening. There was a noise down the rocky slopes. Dodd listened with pricking ears. There was a mist over the hill to reinforce the lessening darkness, and Dodd could see nothing. Then they both heard something, a clash and a clatter, unmistakably like the sound of a horse slipping on the rocks. Dodd was on his feet in one motion, gliding silently off to the flank to investigate the new threat of danger from a safer angle, like a poacher's dog.

He heard the clatter again, and then a voice speaking in Portuguese—the stunted man's voice. Dodd walked towards it, and soon he saw him looming up through the mist, and by his side, elephantine in its appearance in the weird light, a big, raw-boned mule, one-eyed, harness-galled, with flapping lips revealing yellow teeth. The stunted man clapped the mule on the shoulder.

'Food,' he said. He was always a man of few words.

The delighted Dodd saw the commissariat problem solved for days and days. Bernardino came up and grinned broadly. Between them they led the one-eyed mule over the hill down well below the crest, close above the river. Here Dodd judged that the smoke of a fire would be best concealed; in the prevailing mist and rain it would be safe enough here. The stunted man took the knife from his belt and held it to the big artery in the mule's throat; he was about to make the fatal stab when Dodd noticed that the knife was all smeared with dried blood, and so were the stunted man's hand and forearm. Dodd guessed what the blood was—one can rarely steal a mule from a convoy's horse lines without killing at least one sentry. Dodd may have been leading the life of a savage for some time past, but he was not as much a savage as to care to see his meat killed with a weapon stained in that fashion. The other two tried but failed to conceal their amusement at this attitude of his, and Bernardino took the knife, scrambled down to the riverside, and washed it with painful elaboration. Then he brought it back and handed it to the stunted man.

The knife went home among the great blood vessels of the throat, but the mule's convulsive jerk at the prick of the knife caused him to break the halter which tied him to a stump, and his subsequent plunges bade fair to pitch him into the river. The stunted man saw the danger, and, regardless of the lashing hoofs, threw his arms round the mule's neck. When Dodd's plans for the destruction of the bridge are allowed for, it seems permissible to assume that the future course of European history might turn upon the plunging of a harness-galled mule with its throat cut. The stunted man achieved his object. The mule fell with a clash of shod hoofs, but he lay on his side among the rocks and had not fallen into the water. He made one or two unavailing efforts to rise, but the blood spouting in great jets from his severed carotid drained his strength away, and soon he lay still and dead.

Then there was a great business to be done. Dodd gave orders as well as he could.

'Fire,' he said, handing over his precious tinderbox to Bernardino, and then, pointing to the mule, 'Much, much, much.'

Bernardino ran about gathering fuel, and then with flint, tinder, and slow-match set himself to kindle a fire. The stunted man began to flay and remove a quarter of mule. Dodd himself, his military instincts quite ineradicable, went rifle in hand up the hill again to take up a position on 'the table'—ignoring the two dead men who still hung nailed to the thorn tree close beside it—to keep guard lest the smoke of the fire, or pure chance for that matter, should bring up stray parties of the enemy. There was no real need to worry, although he did not know it. Nearly all the battalion billeted in the village were still on the road escorting the bridging train. Only enough sound men remained to guard the sick.

It was a gargantuan feast which that mule provided. Bernardino and the stunted man ate until they could eat no more, and then the stunted man came up the hill to where Dodd was on guard, pointing back to where the fire was, and obviously set himself to keep guard in Dodd's place. He was a far more thoughtful man than Bernardino.

Dodd went back to where Bernardino, all slimed with the mule's blood, was holding great chunks of meat on a ramrod before the fire. Dodd ate gluttonously, and by the time he was satisfied Bernardino found that he had regained a supplementary appetite and was able to start again. Dodd let him eat as much as he could hold; he had a good many days of half rations to make up for and—so Dodd's plans dictated—a good many days of half rations yet to come, against which he might as well make as much preparation as he could. Yet when he simply could hold no more, and the grateful warmth of the fire was tempting him to stretch himself beside it and make up for nights and nights of broken rest, Dodd kept him stirred into activity.

He had to keep on bringing in further supplies of fuel, and assist Dodd in the task of grilling more and more meat. Bernardino's face, no less than Dodd's, was toasted a bright scarlet. The heat of the fire was such that they had to shield their hands from it as they turned the stickfuls of meat before the blaze. It was the most primitive cookery imaginable. Dodd insisted on the meat being very thoroughly roasted, until it was quite dry, in fact, and naturally it became charred at the edges, but that could not be helped. The meat was coarse and tough and fibrous and had a peculiar sweetish flavour, but to men who have been hungry enough to eat raw horse roast mule is a positive luxury.

Anyway, Dodd had never known what good

food was, not once in all his life, nor had Bernardino. It was mere irony that the money and effort wasted in the war in which they were fighting was sufficient to keep every single man engaged in it in Lucullan luxury for all their days.

The pile of roast meat, steaks and succulent chunks from the ribs, grew larger and larger, despite the fact that every now and then both Dodd and Bernardino discovered that they could manage another bite or two of some particularly attractive fragment. Bernardino looked at the colossal pile of meat with wondering eyes; he could not see the reason for it at all. But it was impossible to ask questions. He just went on toasting meat and gathering fuel, all that livelong day. It was not until something over a hundredweight of meat had been cooked that Dodd appeared satisfied, and Bernardino could go to sleep, lying like a cat before the glowing embers of the fire. The warmth and his unwontedly full belly made him sleep for thirteen solid hours, right round until the next morning, in fact.

He woke to find Dodd and the stunted man making evident preparations for a further journey. They were loading themselves with the cooked meat, stuffing every available pouch and pocket with it, and so did Bernardino have to do when he got to his feet. It was a grievous burden which each carried when they started, some forty pounds of meat each. But Dodd was happy. That would mean rations for three weeks provided the meat kept good—or even if it did not, for the matter of that. Maggoty mule meat is better than none at all. Dodd, although he had never heard the expression 'a balanced diet', and although the word 'calory' had not yet been invented, would gladly have exchanged half the meat for an equal weight of bread, but since such an exchange was quite impossible he wasted no regrets over it. That careful cooking of the meat to an extreme point of dryness had for its object the preserving of the meat for the maximum possible time, and it was still cold, although spring was so close at hand.

It was a perilous journey upon which they were setting out, although perforce only Dodd could know its objective. They came down the hill to the main road, and started to pursue the convoy. But here the river and road ran close together in an upstream direction, and the country beside the road was for some way more open and level, and there were troops in the little hamlets which dotted it. Their progress was terribly slow—it was a matter of crawling along ditches, and sneaking furtively from coppice to coppice, and lying concealed for long periods when any of the enemy were in sight.

Yet this was the only way of moving through this country. Stratagems and disguises would have been of no help at all, for such was the state of the war in Portugal that there was no chance of posing as peaceful civilians making a journey for private reasons. There were no peaceful civilians, and private reasons had ceased to exist. The French would hang or shoot—if they did not torture—anyone they caught who was not a Frenchman; they had been doing so for so many weeks in this area that few natives were left, and these were living like wild beasts—like Dodd and his two companions, in fact—in secret lairs.

Nor was the notion of moving along the high road by night any more practicable. There were military posts and villages along it in such numbers as to necessitate incessant detours, and Dodd had far too much sense to contemplate prolonged movement by night across unknown country. They were out of the stunted man's area by now, and Bernardino's muleteer's knowledge of the country could hardly be expected to extend to cover every ditch and thicket. All they could do was to struggle along in the fashion they were following, taking what precautions they could to ensure that on their detours away from the road they did not overshoot the mark and go past the bridging convoy, which with twenty-four hours' start was somewhere ahead of them, destined for a locality which Dodd was very anxious to ascertain.

The chances were against their getting through alive. Dodd had known it when he started, but he had come so far along the road to thinking for himself that he judged it to be his duty to risk his life without orders on an objective chosen by himself rather than preserve it like the one talent, to be given back unprofitably to the regiment when the great day should come when he could rejoin. He guessed that his life was of small importance compared with the bridge the French were building, and so he imperilled it, not cheerfully, but not despondently either; equably is perhaps the best expression, for there was nothing of resignation about Dodd.

The fiendish difficulty of the journey displayed itself at once when they began it, creeping along ditches and furrows. It was dreadfully fatiguing, and the continual tension was trying. Afterwards Dodd could not remember the order of events at all; he could not even remember how many days and nights they had spent on the journey before they were discovered and chased. Yet little things remained printed indelibly on his memory—details like the pattern of the leaves in the patch of undergrowth where they lay hidden half a morning awaiting an opportunity of crossing an exposed stretch of land, and the brown mineral stain of the water of one of the little streams where they were cowering when a picket caught sight of them.

The long, heartbreaking pursuit which followed could not be remembered with the same clarity. It was like a nightmare, recalled as something horrible but blurred in its outline. Dodd remembered the view halloo which greeted them, and the line of shouting Frenchmen which chased them. He remembered how his heart laboured, and how his legs grew weaker and weaker under him while the load on his back grew intolerably heavy. He remembered how a fresh patrol appeared in front of them heading them off, attracted by the yells of the pursuers, and he remembered always what an effort of will was necessary to change the direction of his flight and to urge his weary legs once more to another spurt while he seemed unable to draw another breath or take another step. He remembered Bernardino falling to the ground exhausted, and then the stunted man, and how he had to fight against the temptation to stop with them and end all this toilsome business in one last glorious fight.

He could hardly bring himself to believe it when he found at last that he was no longer pursued, that he had no longer to force one leg in front of the other, that he could fling himself on to the ground and gaspingly regain his breath and wait for the sledge-hammer beating of his heart to subside. When the time came that he could move once more, he crept along to peer through the torn bushes over the crest of the hill to where his late pursuers were gathered round the foot of a tall, isolated tree.

They were hoisting the banners of their triumph, in celebration of having caught two more bandits. Strange flags they were, which mounted up to the horizontal branch, black flags, which flapped in a curious, contorted way. They were Bernardino and the stunted man, his last two friends, no less dear to him despite the fact that of one of them he never knew the name. Apparently the unit which had caught them had kept back from the bridge-builders a supply of rope for the hanging of bandits.

There was sorrow in Dodd's heart as he looked down on the pitiful scene, but it did not prevent him from turning away and setting himself to survey and plan the next adventurous quarter of a mile of his route. There are many who give up, and many who procrastinate, but there are some who go on.

After this the nightmare-like quality of Dodd's Odyssey persisted. There was loneliness to be contended with now; it bore heavily on Dodd in the end. Often he found himself, as he crawled and crept on his way, muttering directions to himself—usually in the baby Portuguese which was all he had spoken during the last months. Loneliness and fatigue and strain and bad food made a strange dark labyrinth of his mind, but they did not prevent him from creeping steadily along on his self-set task. He ate very little of his roast mule meat, for he never seemed hungry, but he still went on.

It must have been the very day when Bernardino was hanged that the cannonade began, to maintain a continual monotonous accompaniment to Dodd's thoughts. It was very distant—a mere dull growling, very far off. But it went on and on and on without a break and without variation. There was only one kind of cannonade which could make that kind of sound—a siege. Somewhere an army was pounding away to bore a hole in a stone wall with cannon-balls while someone else was firing away trying to stop them. Dodd heard the sound, and sometimes stopped to listen to it. But it was away to the south, fifty miles away or more, and whatever it portended it could only make the destruction of the bridge of greater importance than ever. Dodd went on all day, and all the next day, and all the next, with that dull muttering in his ears. So persistent was it that at night-fall when it ceased, his hearing remained at attention, conscious that something was missing.

It was in the afternoon that Dodd reached the Zezere, and it was evening when he set eyes again on the bridging equipment. In a straight line it is twenty-five miles from where Dodd started to Punhete; Dodd's route with all its zigzags and detours must have stretched to fifty—the greater part of which he had done on his hands and knees or on his belly.

CHAPTER NINETEEN

Dodd reached the river unexpectedly and halted in some dismay above its ravine. He had passed several streams already, and had been able to splash through them, but this was a raging river, running white amid its rocks, and apparently impassable. If downstream there were any means of passing, between this point and the confluence with the Tagus, he guessed it must be well guarded by the enemy. If he had to cross he must go upstream, in search either of an unguarded bridge left intact—a most unlikely possibility—or else of a spot where the river grew sufficiently small to cross; as far as the mountains which gave it birth, perhaps. Before he plunged thus into the interior he had better make one of his periodical reconnaissances of the main road, to make sure that he was not leaving the bridging train behind him.

He slid down the nearly vertical fifty-foot bank of the ravine and began to pick his way along the water's edge with the river roaring beside him. It was difficult walking, for the river filled its bed, and the side of the ravine ran nearly vertically down to the water. And at frequent intervals Dodd had to climb this bank to peer over the edge, to look both for the enemy and to see if the high road were yet in sight. As he made his way downstream the sides of the ravine became not merely lower but less sloped. Dodd began to fear that soon he would be deprived of the cover of this deep, natural trench. Indeed, he actually formed the resolution to leave it because the ravine had grown so shallow that it was no shelter at all, but, on the contrary, an added danger. Accessible running water always increased the chance of meeting Frenchmen, who might be there watering horses or washing clothes.

But just as he reached this decision he saw the bridging train. There was no mistaking it, assembled down there on the river bank with just a glint of the Tagus showing in the distance. There were the pontoons, stacked in orderly piles just above the water, and the great masses of timber road-way, and heaps of cables, and Dodd could see men busily at work putting up a low roof over the mass of material, and others above the water hammering away at what Dodd guessed to be runways for lowering the pontoons down to the river.

It was nearly dark by now, and Dodd had but a short time to observe these things. As twilight fell he picked his way upstream again and chose a lair for himself—a stony hollow in the side of the ravine, where he could rest. That night, just as on most of the other nights and most of the days, it rained heavily and a cold wind blew. Dodd still, before going to sleep, found passing through his mind that old Biblical passage about foxes having holes and birds having nests.

Yet if he had been asked—it is quite impossible, but assume it to have happened—if he were happy, he would not have known what to reply. He would have admitted readily enough that he was uncomfortable, that he was cold, and badly fed, and verminous; that his clothes were in rags, and his feet and knees and elbows raw and bleeding through much walking and crawling; that he was in ever-present peril of his life, and that he really did not expect to survive the adventure he was about to thrust himself into voluntarily, but all this had nothing to do with happiness: that was something he never stopped to think about. Perhaps the fact that he did not think about it proves he was happy. He was a soldier carrying out his duty as well as he knew how. He would have been the first to admit that under the wise direction of an officer what he had done and what he proposed to do might be more successful, but as it was he felt (or rather he would have felt if he had thought about it) he had nothing with which to reproach himself. And that condition is not at all far from true happiness. At the same time he would have been utterly astonished if he had ever been told that some day a printed book would devote paragraphs to the consideration of his frame of mind.

The usual shuddering misty morning succeeded the watery dawn, and Dodd stretched to loosen his stiffened joints and peered about for an enemy before making his way down the rushing river again to the point from which he could see the bridge-building preparations. He was terribly aware that he must enter into this adventure as well prepared as possible. He was all alone; if he should fail there was no one now who might repeat the attempt after him. From what he could see time was not of pressing importance. He proposed to devote the whole of today— longer, if necessary—to observing what was before him.

He selected a little embrasure of rocks where he could hope to be quite concealed unless anyone passed very close, and from here he stared down the stream at the bustle going on there. Nearest of all was the actual boat-building section. There were two skeletons of pontoons on which men were busy nailing the strakes. A little farther from the river there were cauldrons boiling over fires, set in the angle between two rough hoardings to screen the work somewhat from the wind. Here men were trying to bend their nearly useless timber into shape. Dodd could not guess what they were about, but he saw that there was fire there, and he gulped with hope when he realized how much that might help him. Beyond that clearly someone was painting the bottom of a pontoon—daubing something over it, anyway, something which was contained in another cauldron which stood there. Farther down were two sheds full of rope, and beyond that again was a rope-walk. Dodd recognized that; he had seen one at work at Dover on one occasion, when he had walked into that town from Shorncliffe Camp. Beyond that there was an immense long pile of timber, neatly squared and stacked, which Dodd guessed must be the roadway, ready for laying across the cables when—if—the pontoons should ever be moored in position.

All day long Dodd watched and stared. It was a difficult task which he was setting himself. He was trying to familiarize himself with everything he could see to such an extent that he would be able to find his way about there in the dark. He marked the route thither, making mental notes of a bush here and a gully there, so that he would be able to pick his way to the workplace from point to point however dark it might be. He watched without fretting and without restlessness; it was a task for which all his education and training—or lack of them—had made him eminently fitted. His uneventful boyhood as an agricultural worker, and his severe schooling in patience during his years as a soldier, were a help now. His mind did not constantly demand new little activities. He could lie and chew the cud of his observations as placidly as a cow.

Yet he redoubled his attention when the long day reached its close. It was important to ascertain if sentries were placed over the work, and if so, how many, and where. When evening fell he saw the workmen cease their labours and troop off up the bank to where a double row of wigwams—rough huts of twigs and branches—awaited them. Then, in the last glimmer of daylight, he saw the guard mounted and the sentries posted. There were only two of them on the works, each of them allotted a beat along half the long line of works. Dodd guessed that they were not there to guard against attack—nothing could be farther from the minds of the French. Knowing the ways of soldiers, he realized that they were posted there to prevent men from stealing the material of the bridge to make fires; the life of a private soldier often resolves itself into one perennial search for fuel, and no soldier is very particular about the source of his supplies. Already Dodd could see the glimmer of fires from among the wigwams.

Dodd might have made his attempt upon the bridge that night, but he exercised his judgement and his patience, and resolved to wait another day. Tonight, exceptionally, there was a moon. It was wan and watery, but it gave sufficient light to add danger to anything he might attempt. He would not be sorry to have the opportunity of a night's watching; he wished to find out all he could about the routine of visiting rounds and sentry changing at this point. With the ordinary French system of outposts he was familiar enough—he had so often done picket duty in the rearguard or advance guard within earshot of the French screen—but he wanted to note all he could tonight. He could see that he might need as much as an hour undisturbed to carry out the plans which his slow but logical brain was constructing.

He stayed on in his hiding-place through the night, dozing for long intervals, but waking up abruptly at every unusual noise. In the clear, still night he could hear everything that went on down there, three hundred yards away. By the time morning came he had all the information he wanted.

Next morning the weather changed again, to a blustering day of much wind and occasional sharp showers, but it was distinctly warmer—a day which was clearly the herald to the coming spring. Dodd still stayed in his hiding-place, lashed at intervals by the rain, but sometimes amazingly warmed and comforted by little spells of sunshine which beat gratefully on his upturned back. When the sun came out he took the opportunity of spreading out his remaining thirteen cartridges to rid them of possible damp. He had taken tremendous care of his ammunition all this winter, but despite all his care he had found two of his cartridges unfit to use. He had no idea how many more might prove to be the same, and, once rammed home, a charge which refused to explode was a crippling nuisance.

Yet Dodd did not allow this simple little duty to interfere with his business of observation. He watched all day long the work down the river. He saw another pontoon completed—the second since he began his watch—and he saw more cable added to the pile in the sheds. In the afternoon he saw two soldiers stagger up from the distant village, each with a cauldron which they put down at the boat-painting place. That would be paint or tar or grease, obviously—if it had been merely water the cauldrons would have been filled from the river. That was helpful for his plans, and he saw no new development which might interfere with them.

When night came he ate temperately of his dried mule meat. He had to force himself to eat at all. Partly it was because even the stolid, philosophic Dodd could feel excitement sometimes, as when about to embark upon an adventure of this sort; partly it was because he had eaten nothing except cold roast mule for a week now; partly it was because the meat, never very attractive in the first place, was by now beginning to grow even more unpleasant. All the same, Dodd made himself eat, because he did not know when he would eat again should he survive the night's adventure. He emptied his pack and his pockets of their en-cumbering stores, and laid them on the ground in his hiding-place. He might be able to return for them, or he might not. It was a harder struggle to decide to leave his rifle. No good soldier ever parts from his weapon; without it, in fact, he ceases to be a soldier. That is a tradition which has come down from prehistoric wars. It irked Dodd sadly to leave his rifle behind. The act of leaving it, besides, indicated too surely that he was going to do his work with his bayonet used like a knife, which savoured strongly of assassination and unsoldierly warfare. Yet the fact remained that the rifle would be an encumbrance, while if he had to use it it would only be because his attempt had failed. It would be far wiser to leave it behind. And because it was wiser, Dodd did so, in the end.

He slid the frog of his bayonet-scabbard along his belt until the weapon hung in the middle of his back; in that position it was least likely to catch or clatter while crawling over rocks. He saw that the bayonet lay free in the scabbard, he made certain that his precious tinder-box was in his pocket, and then he started on his adventure.

He kept to the brink of the river, as offering the route most likely to be clear of the enemy. He crawled on his poor sore elbows and knees over the sharp rocks. The appearance of the moon from behind a cloud kept him motionless in a gully for nearly an hour until it went in again. The flying clouds which obscured the moon brought more than darkness; they brought a sharp spatter of rain which gave him splendid cover for the remainder of his crawl. Finally he settled down, not moving a finger, stretched on his face, behind some low rocks only twenty yards from the end of the sentry's beat.

There he waited; it was not yet midnight, and he could afford to spend several hours in awaiting the best possible combination of circumstances. It was nervous work. At fairly regular intervals he could hear the measured step of the sentry approaching him, and then receding again. Sometimes there would be a pause before the sentry turned back along his beat. That was agonizing, for Dodd, lying on his face, could not tell whether the sentry had halted to rest, and to gaze at the turbulent stream rushing by, or whether he was staring at the dark mass behind the rocks making up his mind that it was human and hostile. But he was not discovered, and sometimes there was a blessed interval of relief from tension when the sentry was at the other end of his beat chatting with his fellow.

The hours stole by; the sentries were twice relieved. Dodd was almost beginning to wonder whether it might not be better if he were to act at once, when the first thing he was waiting for occurred. One of the sentries challenged sharply, the *'Qui vive?'* ringing through the night. The challenge was peaceably replied to. It was the officer of the day on his rounds. Dodd settled himself to wait a little longer; events were working out satisfactorily. A quarter of an hour later came another challenge. This time it was the sergeant with the relief. Dodd heard the sentries changed and the guard march off again. He waited very keyed up now. It was his business to judge of sufficient passage of time for all to be quiet again; it is hard to estimate the passage of twenty minutes when one has nothing whatever to do during that time.

Finally, he waited until the sentry's step was receding, and then he went forward silently to where another rock twenty yards farther on lay close by where the sentry would pass on his return. He drew his sword bayonet and crouched there. He heard the sentries exchange a few words, and then he tautened up his muscles in readiness. Then, as the sentry came near, he sprang, silent and swift, like a leopard.

The rifle regiment sword bayonet was an ideal weapon for silent assassination, long and sharp and slender, curving a little at the tip. Dodd thrust upward with it, with all the strength of his arm. It went up under the sentry's ribs, through his liver and diaphragm, upwards until the long, slender point burst the great blood-vessels beside the heart. Private

Dubois, of the fourth battalion of the Forty-Sixth, died without even a groan. He died on his feet. Dodd's left hand grasped the stock of Dubois' sloped musket; his right hand quitted the bayonet's hilt and his arm shot round the man's waist in time to catch him as he fell and to ease him to the ground without a sound.

That disposed of one sentry. Dodd stooped and with fierce effort tore the bayonet from the corpse, and thrust it back, dripping as it was, into the scabbard. Then he picked up the Frenchman's heavy musket with its fixed bayonet, and started back with sloped arms down the sentry's beat. He stopped in the darkness behind the shed; the other sentry, as he approached, could see only a dark, erect figure and the glimmer of a bayonet as Dodd stood at ease. Nothing could have been farther from his thoughts than that it was an Englishman who stood there and not his acquaintance Dubois, whom he had last seen only two minutes ago. He said something as he came up. Presumably his last thought must have been that Dubois had suddenly gone mad, as the dark figure stepped forward and brought the musket butt crashing down on his head.

There was less need for silence to kill only a single sentry, and the butt is more certain than the bayonet to ensure instant inability to give warning. Such was the strength with which Dodd struck that the musket stock broke at the small of the butt; the heavy base, attached now by only a few fibres, waggled heavily as Dodd brought the weapon back ready if another blow were needed.

None was. The man had fallen instantly. Dodd's expression hardened in the darkness as he stooped over him. Soldiers do not kill wounded men, but in this case, with the fate of a campaign dependent on a man's silence, Dodd would not have hesitated at the cutting of a throat. But it was not necessary; the man's brains were running out of his shattered skull like porridge.

Dodd was free now to go on with his plan. The visiting rounds had been made; sentries would not be changed for nearly two hours. An hour ought to be sufficient for the completion of his work. He listened intently for an instant to see if the dull sounds had caught the attention of the soldiers up the bank. He heard nothing, and he burst into rapid action. He hurried round to the river front of the works. In the cable sheds he found masses of loosely twisted, hairy rope, and with his sword bayonet he cut an armful of two-feet lengths of this. Then he groped his way to where he had seen put down the cauldrons of liquid for daubing the bottoms of the pontoons. There was still plenty in them. By touch Dodd ascertained that their contents was a semi-liquid grease that ought to burn furiously. He soaked his lengths of rope in the stuff, and put them among the stacked pontoons.

Cutting himself a fresh supply he soaked these too. There was still place for some more among the pontoons. The others he took along to the piled road-bed timber; pushed his oily wicks among the planks. For a second he debated the risks of delay against the advantages of more inflammables, and decided that delay was justifiable, so he cut yet more lengths of rope, soaked them, and thrust them among the timber. Then he poured what was left in one cauldron over a pile of pontoons, and what was left in the other over some of the mass of rope in the shed. Then he went up the bank to where he had seen the fires. Digging with his foot among the ashes disclosed a mass of red embers. They would save him a good deal of trouble with all the paraphernalia of flint and steel and tinder and slow-match.

He tore off his battered old shako, shovelled embers into it with his foot, and ran, clumsily yet fast, down to the sheds. He poured the embers out on to the oil-soaked cables. That ought to make a fine blaze. The cables were the easiest stuff to burn, and if they were destroyed Dodd guessed that they would be difficult to replace, so that their destruction might be equivalent to the destruction of the whole bridge. The oil spluttered and sizzled; there rose to his nostrils a smell like the frying he had often noticed in Portuguese kitchens. Then a wisp of cable took fire; the little flame sprang up, sank, sprang up again, and spread to the whole thickness of the cable, which burnt like a torch. Dodd watched it for a moment, watched the flame spread to the other ropes and then, catching up a burning length, he raced along the works with it. He stopped wherever he remembered having inserted a piece of oily rope, which he lit. They burnt nobly. Soon all along the heaped masses of timber, and among the stacked pontoons there were little roaring flames. From the time of the first bringing of the fire until now not more than five minutes had elapsed.

It was at this moment that there came a shout and a bustle from the bank where the French were, and Dodd knew that he had no more time for destruction. He flung his torch in among the pontoons, and ran away in the darkness upstream. If he had had his rifle with him he might have stayed longer, firing a shot or two to keep the French back so that the flames might gain a better hold, but his rifle was up in his hiding-place. And a glance at the piled cables just before he fled showed him that it was not necessary: the sheds were a roaring furnace already. The sight of that mass of flames cheered Dodd immensely as he ran for his life up the river bank. The men who were now rushing down at top speed to the works would find that blaze hard to extinguish. From the French huts came the long roll of a drum.

CHAPTER TWENTY

It was after the bridge-builders had been established for two days on the banks of the Zezere that the faint sound of a distant bombardment came to their ears. It was a very distant droning noise, coming from far away to the south, and everyone could guess from the quality of the sound that it implied a siege. Exactly which town was being besieged, and who was besieging and who besieged, no one in the ranks could really guess. Not even the men of the Second and Sixth Corps in their marchings to and fro across Spain had ever been led south of the Tagus, and a knowledge of Spanish geography beyond the river was not very usual among them. It was Colonel Gille, in command of the bridging party under the general command of General Éblé, who supplied an explanation.

'That sounds like your uncle, sergeant,' he said to Sergeant Godinot, in an interval of inspecting the work on the pontoons.

'Oh, yes, colonel?' said Godinot.

'That must be the Army of Andalusia besieging Badajoz,' said Colonel Gille. 'They are on the move at last. But—'

Colonel Gille bit his sentence off sharply, and swallowed the end. Not even the loose discipline of the French army, which permitted of quite free conversation between a colonel and a sergeant, quite allowed the sergeant to ask questions of the colonel. Godinot could not press Colonel Gille to continue his sentence, but that 'but' had told him a great deal. He could only wait for the colonel to resume his conversation.

'Your uncle is a fine officer,' went on Colonel Gille. 'I knew him well when I was on the Prince of Eckmühl's staff in Poland. I would give something to see his brigade come marching up to the other side of the river. If only the Duke of Dalmatia—'

Colonel Gille left another sentence unfinished.

'Oh, well, we shall see, we shall see,' he concluded lamely before going off to another part of the works. 'This is good work you have been doing here, sergeant.'

Sergeant Godinot, even if he could not divine the details of Colonel Gille's thoughts, could at least guess that the sound of the bombardment of Badajoz was not as comforting to the staff as might be supposed. It proved that the Army of Soult (the Duke of Dalmatia, as Colonel Gille punctiliously called him) was on the move, but it proved also that the move would be an ineffective one. Instead of marching with all his army to their aid, Soult had merely thrust a detachment of his army into the nest of fortresses guarding Southern Portugal. He was besieging Badajoz now. If he was successful in his attack there, he would next have to take Elvas, which was a larger and a better designed and a better garrisoned fortress. And after that there were half a dozen smaller fortresses—Albuquerque, Olivenza, and so on. It would be months before he could appear on the Tagus by this route. Months? And the French army there was dying of sheer starvation, at the rate of hundreds a day. No wonder that the sound of the distant bombardment was the knell of the hopes of the French staff.

Sergeant Godinot could not guess these details, of course, but he could guess that there was despair at headquarters, and so could his fellow-soldiers; if confirmation was needed it was supplied by the fact that the miserable daily rations were being reduced even below their previous unhealthy standard. On their first arrival on the Zezere the men used to take their muskets and go out into the neighbouring country and shoot little birds, using bags of tiny stones in place of small shot, but the practice was discontinued almost at once by general order. The army, with no reserves of ammunition, could not waste powder on sparrows, nor even on thrushes. Ragged, barefooted, hungry, and diseased, the French army in Portugal was in imminent danger of going to pieces.

Still, despite the rumours of retreat which sped through the ranks, the bridge building still went on. The carpenters still laboured over their unpromising material, and the rope-makers still twisted cables, and the boat-builders still built boats. The work was very nearly complete now, and everyone knew that even when it was finished they would still have to stand by to lay the bridge when the time came. The men dragged on their uncomfortable existence in the huts above the river, the officers their hardly less uncomfortable existence in houses in the village, save for the officer of the day, for whose use the men built a wooden shed at the end of their row of huts, next door to that devoted to the guard.

Naturally, guard duty was not heavy. In daytime two sentries out on the hill, and at night two additional ones to guard the bridging material from the pilferings to be expected of men chronically short of fuel, were all that were necessary. Fifteen men and a sergeant and a drummer supplied these guards—it was only once in three weeks that a man's turn came round.

The day when Sergeant Godinot was sergeant of the guard had begun no differently from any other. True, a messenger had come from Santarem to summon General Éblé to headquarters—the orderly had told them his message, and they had seen the general ride off—but that might not mean anything of importance. The duties of the sergeant of the guard at this point were not in the least onerous. There were no drunkards to be dealt with, for not one of the men had drunk anything except water for six weeks. Equipment inspections brought no defaulters, for every man's equipment had been reduced by wear and tear to a nullity. Desertion was impossible on this wing of the army; no man would willingly leave the frying pan of life in the ranks for the fire of capture by the irregulars—the English were far away. All that Sergeant Godinot had to do was to post his sentries and relieve them at the proper time. The rest of the time he could sit and doze at the doorway of the guard hut while his men snored away their four hours off duty inside.

Night came with a gusty wind and showers of rain and an intermittent moon. Everything was very quiet in the camp. From where Godinot was sitting he could just hear the gurgle and splash of the turbulent Zezere. He had ample time to sit and meditate on his hunger, and to try to work out what would be the future course of the campaign, and to look back on the golden days when he had been a schoolboy in Nantes, sailing boats on Sundays, and with always enough to eat and with never a tear in his clothes lasting for more than a day. His shako was on his knees, and he smoothed his scalp thoughtfully—before he had been promoted and transferred to the new fourth battalion he had served in the grenadier company, and the bearskin of the grenadiers tended to make a man's hair thin on top. The last change of sentries had left young Dubois on guard down by the river. Godinot hoped that Dubois would come safely through the campaign. All the others—Boyel and little Godron and Fournier and the rest—were dead. And he knew all their mothers in Nantes—women who would weep and would say he was to blame. The poor women did not know yet that their sons were dead, although it was as much as three months since Boyel was killed. They never would know as long as the army remained isolated here in Portugal. But that could not last much longer. Soon they must move—and Godinot found his thoughts beginning to circle again. He shook them off and rose to his feet, glancing at the guardhouse watch—the one watch which remained in working order in the whole detachment—hanging on the wall. There was still an hour before sentries had to be changed again. He stepped out into the night, stopped, rubbed his eyes, and looked again.

Down on the river's brink there was a dull red glow like a fire. On each side of it were a row of twinkling points of light, like candles. As he watched, one of these points of light expanded and brightened and reddened. There was another point of light moving about down there. Someone was setting fire to the bridge—the bridge was on fire already!

'Guard, turn out!' roared Godinot. 'Turn out, you bastards. Quick!'

He kicked the men awake as they turned over sleepily. He grabbed the drummer by the collar and stood him, still half-asleep, on his feet.

'Beat to arms! Do you hear me? Beat to arms! Come on, you others.'

He dashed down the slope with the sleepy guard trailing behind. As he ran, he saw tall flames shoot up from the cable sheds. As a gust of wind blew, the sound of the burning rose to a roar. Then he tripped and fell with a crash over a dead body. He paid it no attention, but plunged on to try to save the precious bridge.

The cables were the most precious, and were burning the strongest. He plunged into the mass of flames, and tried to drag the stuff out, but the heat drove him back. He turned to the men who came up behind him.

'Buckets! Water!' he said. 'Use your hats— anything.'

Up the bank the roll of the drum roused sleeping soldiers. Soon they were all pouring down to the river. Men ran with buckets, with cooking cauldrons. A bucket chain—a double bucket chain—was formed from the river's brink to the rope sheds. But it was not with mere bucketfuls of water that that blaze could be extinguished. Men dragged out masses of burning rope and tried to beat out the flames with bits of wood. But there was so much to do. There were flames roaring up the sides of stacks of pontoons. The timber for the road-bed—dry brittle stuff—was burning in its huge piles, each the size of a cottage. Gusts of wind were carrying sparks everywhere. Men with crowbars tried to tear the great heaps to pieces and roll the burning stuff down the bank, but that was stopped after two great masses of timber had been swept away to be lost in the wide waters of the Tagus. Timber adrift in the Tagus would be as much lost to the French as if it had been burned.

The officers had come running up from their billets in Punhete in all stages of undress and helped to direct the efforts of the men, with Colonel Gille in chief command. The heat and smoke were terrible—at one time and another there were as many as a score of men stretched out on the bank recovering from their effects. No one in the mad struggle noticed the coming of the dawn. No one paid any attention to the despatch rider, who turned up in the middle of the confusion calling for Colonel Gille. The colonel merely snatched the note and crammed it into his pocket before plunging into the battle with the flames again.

They got the fire under at last, but it was a hopeless sight on which their eyes rested in the bleak light of the early morning. Quite three-quarters of the cable were burned, and half the pontoons; the other half were burned in patches where flames had licked up the sides of the stacks of pontoons. Pontoons with one side burned off lay about here and there above the water's edge. A little tangle of rope represented all that remained of the heaps of neat coils which had lain in the sheds. A good deal of the road-bed timber remained, but that was the most easily replaced of all. Taking it all in all, the bridge was utterly ruined. To rebuild it would call for much time—and all available materials had already been used.

The men and the officers, utterly worn out, lay about exhausted on the bank, looking gloomily at the charred remains. No one said anything, no one did anything. Gloom and depression had settled upon them all. No one even stirred when white-haired old General Éblé came trotting up the slope on his emaciated horse. They looked dully at him as he cast his eyes hither and thither over the scene of destruction. Sergeant Godinot was too tired and sick at heart even to feel the apprehension which as sergeant of the guard he ought to have felt. With Dubois dead he had no heart for anything. Colonel Gille and the other officers rose to their feet as General Éblé rode up, and stood shakily at attention. Everyone heard what the general said.

'There is still a lot of timber, boats, rope, all over the place. Why have you left them like this?'

Colonel Gille's teeth showed white in his smoke-blackened face as his lips writhed at this bitter irony.

'Yes, my general,' was all he was able to say.

'Do you call this complete destruction, Colonel Gille? It is as well I came here to see that my orders were obeyed.'

Colonel Gille could only stand to attention and try to take this chastisement unmoved.

'Come on, speak up, man. The men ought to have been on the move an hour ago. Why did you not finish your work?'

By this time doubt had begun to display itself in the expressions of the sapper officers. In this nightmare campaign anything might happen. The general might be mad, or they themselves might be mad.

'Oh, for God's sake, colonel,' snapped General Éblé, showing anger at last. 'Pull yourself together, man, and your men too. Why have you not obeyed my orders?'

'Orders?' repeated Colonel Gille stupidly.

'I sent you orders three hours back that the bridge was to be burnt down to the last stick and the bridging detachment returned to their units. The army retreats tomorrow.'

A lightning change came over the officers' faces. Even Colonel Gille smiled. With a flash of recollection he put his hand in his pocket and pulled out the despatch which had been handed him in the middle of the rush to extinguish the flames.

'Get these pontoons stacked together again,' he ordered briefly. 'Bring that rope and pile the whole lot together and burn it. And set fire to the roadway timber again. You see, it was like this, my general—'

But there is no need to follow Colonel Gille into the ramifications of his explanation to General Éblé on how the bridge came to be set on fire prematurely and extinguished again. When an army is about to set out on a dangerous retreat in face of an active enemy there is little time for explanation.

Once more the crackle and roar of the flames made themselves heard above the gurgle of the river, and the wind blew a long streamer of smoke across the countryside. Soon all that was left of the bridge on which hundreds of men had laboured for three months was a long row of piles of white ashes, still smoking a little.

Down on the high road there was already a long string of artillery marching down towards the concentration point at Santarem. They were the guns which had been brought up to be set in batteries at the confluence of the rivers to cover that hypothetical crossing.

After the guns went the two battalions of infantry who had been waiting here for the same purpose. It was easy to see that they were intended to be battalions, for each was divided into six companies, and of each six one company wore the bearskins of grenadiers and one company the green plumes of the *voltigeurs*. Had it not been for that it might have been guessed that the column represented a single battalion, so short was it. That was the effect of a winter without food.

General Éblé pointed down to the moving column and spoke to Colonel Gille.

'Hurry up and give these men their orders, colonel,' he said. 'They ought to have left before those. Now half of them will never reach their regiments.'

It took some time to issue *feuilles de route* to every non-commissioned officer in charge of a detachment. Nearly every regiment in the French army was represented in the bridge-building column. However, there were no rations to be issued as well, the army staff could not be expected to have sent up from their non-existent store rations for men who were to march in towards them that very day. It was long past noon now, and none of the men had eaten since the day before, and now they were faced with marches of twenty miles or more. No wonder there was gloom upon the faces of the men as they marched off.

Sergeant Godinot's party was the worst of all. Its twenty men (there had been thirty at one time; the other ten lay in the graves where sickness had overtaken them) were at once weak in body and mutinous in soul. The unfortunate sum of their military experiences— they were only one-year conscripts, after all—

had left them without any more desire to serve their country at all. Already Godinot had caught bits of conversation among them which proved that their one ambition was to desert to the English—they would have deserted to the Portuguese if there was the least chance of doing so and surviving. And the very last thing they wanted to do was to march back with the French army through the awful mountains they already knew too well, with the English pressing on their rear and the hated irregulars all round them. Yet as they were all of them still only boys who had not yet attained their full growth the months of underfeeding and exposure had left them very weak, and such was their present hunger that they could hardly stagger along. Some of them, however, retained just enough spirit to burst into hoots and catcalls when General Éblé and the other officers rode past them, overtaking them on the road towards Santarem. Sergeant Godinot could not check them.

Sergeant Godinot reflected ruefully that he had to march these men twenty-five miles before dawn next morning, with the prospect of another march, and perhaps even a battle, immediately on arrival. With Dubois dead, there was no one in the detachment he could trust. It was going to be a difficult time for him. He would be glad when he got into Nossa Senhora do Rocamonde—that, he learned for the first time from his *feuille de route*, was the surprising name of the village where the Forty-Sixth had lain so long billeted.

The march was far worse than he anticipated. The whisperings that went on in the ranks behind him boded no good, he knew. He guessed that the men were realizing that twenty men, banded together, might be safe from the irregulars and be able to find their way to the English outposts. He might at any moment be faced with mutiny. Certainly he was faced all the time with disobedience to orders and with mutinous arguments. The men kept calling out that they were tired, they kept asking for rests, and when a rest was granted they were sulky about starting again. Godinot had to plead and urge and beg. He did not dare use violent methods. Even although military law justified him in threatening to shoot those who disobeyed, the situation did not. At the first sign of a physical threat he would have found a bayonet through him or a bullet in his brain. If there had been even one man among them whom he could trust, one man to guard his back, he might have cowed and overawed those mutinous dogs. As it was he could only plead and joke, and pretend to ignore the *sotto voce* insolences which reached his ears.

After dark the trouble became much worse, naturally. Sergeant Godinot marched at the tail of the little column, slipping and stumbling over the stones. He urged them along, keeping an eye open lest any should take advantage of the darkness to leave the ranks. He tried to cheer them up by drawing vivid pictures of the rations which would be issued to them when they reached the battalion—but that was not successful. The men remembered what sort of rations had been issued before they were detailed to the bridging train, and they could form a shrewd guess as to what they would be like now, after two months' further starvation.

The moment came when the whole section flung themselves down on the roadside and swore they could not move another step—not for all the sergeants in Christendom. Godinot did his best. He reached into the darkness and seized what he thought to be the ringleader by the collar and hauled him to his feet, and then the man next to him, and then the next. If he had been an unpopular man they might have killed him then, but, as it was, they spared his life in the scuffle which flared up there at the side of the road. Somebody kicked Godinot; somebody pushed him back. Somebody else, more vicious, took his musket by the muzzle and swung the butt end round in the darkness close to the ground, like a scythe. It was a blow delivered with all the lout's strength; it hit Godinot on the leg and he fell with a cry. Then they all ran off in a body, like a pack of schoolboys (they were hardly more than that) detected on a piece of mischief, leaving Godinot on his knees on the road, trying to get to his feet.

Godinot found that even when he managed to get on his feet he could not long retain the position. The small bone of his right leg was broken; it was agony to walk or even to stand. He could only make the slowest possible progress along the road, and the others never came back to help him. What happened to them, whether they eventually rejoined their battalion, or achieved their ambition of deserting to the English, or died of starvation, or fell into the hands of the Portuguese, will never be known.

After two days the Portuguese irregulars found Godinot. Terrible creatures these Portuguese were—half naked, reduced to skeletons by starvation, as mad with rage at their sufferings and those of their country as was Godinot with pain and hunger and thirst when they found him. They had come creeping across the Zezere, closing in remorselessly on the French army when it gathered itself together to make its retreat. Godinot was the first of the stragglers they picked up, and he was not to be the last by any manner of means. Although he was crazy when they found him, they did not spare his life.

CHAPTER TWENTY-ONE

Rifleman Dodd was not disturbed in the hiding-place to which he fled after setting fire to the bridge. Even if anyone had seen him as he ran away when the alarm was given they were all too busy fighting the fire to trouble about a single fugitive. Dodd reached the shelter of the rocks, and assured himself that his rifle and the rest of his gear were there. In his hand he found, rather to his astonishment, that he still held the battered remnants of his shako. It had been so soaked with rain that the glowing embers had only burned one or two small holes in it. He pulled it on again over his mop of hair and passed the chin strap over the tangle of his beard. Down the stream he could see the flames of the burning bridge, with the figures of the fire-fighting party rushing about round them like old-fashioned pictures of devils in hell.

He watched their exertions with as much excitement as his exhausted condition would allow, and the longer the fire burned the more assured he could become that his efforts had been successful. He felt some elation, but not nearly as much as he would have done had he been fresh and strong and fit. Indeed, now that his efforts had been crowned with success, he was mainly conscious only of weariness, and of something which oppressed him like despair. It was home-sickness—not the desire for the green Sussex Downs, but the desire to be once more with his regiment, marching along with the green-clad files, exchanging jagged jests with his fellows, squatting round the camp fires, leading a life fatalistically free from anxiety and responsibility.

He had almost to force himself to take an interest in the scene of ruin which daylight disclosed—the heaps of ashes, the half-burned boats, the exhausted bridging train lying about the ruins of their handiwork in attitudes clearly indicative of despair. His interest revived when later in the day he saw guns and infantry on the move downstream along the distant high road, and when the bridging party pulled themselves together and wearily set about the task of piling together the debris of the bridge and completing the destruction. All this looked uncommonly like the beginnings of a retreat. Then the bridging party began to march away in small detachments, some by the high road, others by the two paths running diagonally inland from the village. The last to leave were a group of mounted officers and orderlies, and when they had gone the banks of the stream were left desolate, with only the great heaps of smoking ashes to mark where had been the farthest limits of the French army.

Certainly these moves indicated a

concentration, and a concentration could only mean one of two things—an attack on the Lines or a retreat. Dodd knew far too much about the condition of the French army to consider an attack on the Lines in the least possible. There only remained a retreat—and he can hardly be blamed for believing, with a modest pride, that it was he who had caused the French army to retreat. And a retreat meant that he would soon have his path cleared for rejoining his regiment, and that prospect caused him far more excitement than did the consideration of his achievements. He had to compel himself to remain where he was until next day, and then, with all due precaution, he started back across country— over much the same route as he had previously followed largely on his hands and knees—back towards Santarem.

What he saw confirmed him in his theory of an immediate retreat. The French had burned the villages and hamlets in which they had found shelter through the winter, just as the Germans were to do, in France one hundred and six years later. They burnt everything, destroyed everything; the smoke of their burnings rose to the sky, wherever one looked. In truth, the area which the French had occupied was horrible with its burnt villages and its desolate fields, ruined and overgrown, where not a living creature was to be seen. There were dead ones enough to compensate—dead men and dead animals, some already skeletons, some bloated corpses, with a fair sprinkling of dead men—and women—swinging from trees and gallows here and there. Yet it was all just a natural result, even if a highly coloured one, of war, and war was a natural state, and so the horrible landscape through which Dodd trudged did not depress him unduly—how could it when he was on the way back to his regiment?

As for the wake of death which Dodd had left behind him—the Frenchmen whose deaths he had caused or planned, the Portuguese who had died in his sight or to his knowledge, from the idiot boy of his first encounter to Bernardino and the stunted man a week ago, all that made no impression at all upon Dodd. Five campaigns had left him indifferent regarding the lives of Portuguese or Frenchmen.

Santarem when Dodd reached it was a mere wreck of a town—only as much remained of it as there remains of a fallen leaf when spring comes round. And just beyond Santarem Dodd met the first English patrol; the English were out of the Lines. Great minds sometimes think alike: the conclusions reached by Marshal the Prince of Essling and General Lord Wellington had been identical. The former had judged that his army was too weak to remain where it was on the very day that the latter had issued orders for his army to sally forth and fall upon the weakened French. Advance and retreat exactly coincided. The Light Dragoons came pushing up the road on the heels of the French from one direction just when Dodd came down it in the other.

The lieutenant in command of the patrol looked at Dodd curiously.

'Who in God's name do you think you are?' he asked.

Dodd thrilled at the sound of the English language, yet when he tried to speak he found difficulty; he had spent months now struggling with a foreign language.

'Dodd,' he said at length. 'Rifleman, Ninety-Fifth, sir.'

The lieutenant stared down at him; he had seen some strange sights during the war, but none stranger than this. An incredibly battered and shapless shako rested precariously on the top of a wild mane of hair; beneath it a homely English face burnt to a red-black by continual exposure, and two honest blue English eyes looked out through a bristling tangle of beard all tawny-gold. With the British army Dodd shared the use of a razor with Eccles, his front rank man; with the Portuguese Dodd had never once set eyes on a razor. The green tunic and trousers were torn and frayed so that in many places the skin beneath could be seen, and only fragments of black braid remained, hanging by threads, and there were toes protruding through the shoes. Yet the lieutenant's keen eye could detect nothing important as missing. The rifle in the man's hand looked well cared for, the long sword bayonet was still in its sheath. His equipment seemed intact, with the cartridge pouches on the belt and what must have been the wreck of a greatcoat in its slings on his back. The lieutenant's first inward comment on seeing Dodd had been 'Deserter'—desertion being the plague of a professional army—but deserters do not come smiling up to the nearest patrol, nor do they bring back all their equipment. Besides, men did *not* desert from the Ninety-Fifth.

'Are you trying to rejoin your battalion?' asked the lieutenant.

'Yessir,' said Dodd.

'M'm,' said the lieutenant, and then, slowly making up his mind, 'they're only two miles away, on the upper road. Sergeant Casey!'

'Yes, sir.'

'Take this man up to the Ninety-Fifth. Report to Colonel Beckwith.'

The sergeant walked his horse forward, and Dodd stood at his side. The lieutenant snapped an order to the rest of the patrol, and he and his men went jingling forward along the main road, leaving Dodd and his escort to take the by-lane up to the other wing of the advance guard.

The sergeant sat back in his saddle well contented, and allowed his horse to amble quietly up the lane, while Dodd strode along beside him. They exchanged no conversation, for the sergeant was more convinced than his officer had been that Dodd was a deserter, while Dodd's heart was far too full for words. The sun was breaking through the clouds, and it bore a genial warmth, the certain promise of the coming Spring. Away to their left a long column of troops was forming up again after a rest; it was the First Division, for the leading brigade were the Guards in their bearskins and scarlet. Dodd saw the drum-major's silver staff raised, he saw the drummers poise their sticks up by their mouths, and he heard the crash of the drums as the sticks fell. 'Br-rr-rrm, Br-rr-rm' went the drums. Then faintly over the ravaged fields came the squealing of the fifes:

> Some talk of Alexander,
> And some of Hercules,
> Of Hector and Lysander,

as the river of scarlet and black and gold came flooding down the lane. Farther off more troops were in movement; a kilted regiment heading a column marching over a low rise of ground. The sun gleamed on the musket barrels, and the plumes fluttered as the long line of kilts swayed in unison. Dodd breathed in the sunshine with open mouth as he looked about him; he was well content.

They found the Ninety-Fifth on the upper

road, just as the lieutenant had said. They were drawn up on the roadside waiting for the word to move, because for once in a way the foremost skirmishing line had been entrusted to the Fifty-Second and the Portuguese. Sergeant Casey brought his man up to where Colonel Beckwith with his adjutant and other officers stood at the side of the column, with their horses held by orderlies.

'What's this? What's this?' demanded the colonel. Beckwith, the beloved colonel of the Ninety-Fifth, was popularly known as 'Old What's this?' because that was how he prefaced every conversation.

The sergeant told him as much as he knew.

'Very good, sergeant, that'll do,' said Beckwith, and the sergeant saluted and wheeled his horse and trotted back, while Beckwith watched him go. If there was any dirty linen to wash, the Ninety-Fifth would not do it in front of strangers.

'Well, who the devil are you?' demanded Beckwith, at last.

'Dodd, sir. Rifleman. Mr Fotheringham's company.'

'*Captain* Fotheringham's company,' corrected Beckwith absentmindedly, Apparently there had been some promotion this winter.

The colonel ran his eye up and down Dodd's remarkable uniform. Just as the lieutenant had done, he was taking note of the fact that the man seemed to have done his best

241

to keep his equipment together.

'Dodd,' said Colonel Beckwith to himself. He was one of those officers who know the name and record of every man in the ranks. 'Let me see. Why, yes, Matthew Dodd. I remember you. You enlisted at Shorncliffe. But you look more like Robinson Crusoe now.'

There was a little splutter of mirth at that from the adjutant and the other officers in the background, for the comparison was extraordinarily apt, save in Dodd's eyes, for he had never heard of Robinson Crusoe.

'What happened to you?' asked the colonel. He tried to speak sternly, because the man might be a deserter, as the sergeant had tried to hint, although men did *not* desert from the Ninety-Fifth.

'I was cut off, sir, when we were retreating to the Lines,' said Dodd, still finding it hard to speak. 'Been out here trying to rejoin ever since.'

'Out here?' repeated the colonel, looking round at the desolation all about them. That desolation was in itself a sufficient excuse for the state of the man's uniform. And the man looked at him honestly, and despite himself the colonel could never help softening to the pleasant Sussex burr whenever he heard it.

'Is there anyone who can answer for you?' asked the colonel.

'Dunno, sir. Perhaps Mr—Captain Fotheringham—sir—'

'I can remember when you were reported missing, now you remind me,' said the colonel musingly. 'Matthew Dodd. Nothing on your sheet. Five years enlisted. Vimiero. Corunna. Flushing. Talavera. Busaco.'

The glorious names fell one by one from the colonel's lips, but the colonel was being matter-of-fact: he did not realize what a marvellous opportunity this was to sentimentalize.

'Yes, sir,' said Rifleman Dodd.

'You mean you want to fall in now?' asked the colonel. 'You'll have to go back to the advanced depot.'

The great wave of relief in Dodd's soul was instantly flattened by the realization that he could not rejoin at once.

'Oh, sir,' said Dodd. It took more courage to protest to the colonel than it did to burn the Frenchmen's bridge. 'Can't I—can't—'

'You mean you want to fall in now?' asked the colonel.

'Yes, sir. Please, sir.'

'Oh, well, I suppose you can. Report to the quartermaster this evening and tell him I said you were to have another pair of shoes and a coat and trousers to hide your nakedness. And for God's sake have that hair and beard off by tomorrow morning.'

'Yes, sir. Thank you, sir.'

Dodd was about to salute when the colonel checked him.

'What happened to you all this time?' he asked curiously. 'How did you live? What did you get up to?'

'Dunno, sir. I managed somehow, sir.'

'I suppose you did,' said Beckwith thoughtfully. He realized he would never know any details. There might even be an epic somewhere at the back of all this, but he would never be able to induce these dumb Sussex men to tell it. 'Very well, you can fall in. Join your old company for the present.'

The epic would have to wait long before it would be written. It would only be pieced together with much difficulty, from hints in diaries here and there—diaries of French officers and English riflemen. Dodd would never tell it in its entirety. Sometimes little bits of it would come out over the camp fire, on a long evening when the brandy ration had been larger than usual or someone had looted a quart or two of the wine of the country, and would be noted by some of the many diarists to be found in the ranks of the Rifle Brigade. Many years later, when Dodd was a rheumaticky old pensioner, mumbling in approaching senility in the chimney corner, he would tell bits of the tale to the doctor and the Squire's young son, but he never learned to tell a story straight, and the tale of how he altered history—as he thought—was always so broken up among reminiscences of Waterloo and the storming of Badajoz that it was hard to disentangle. Not that it mattered. Not even trifles depended on it, for in those days there were no medals or crosses for the men in the ranks. There was only honour and duty, and it was hard for a later generation to realize that these abstractions had meant anything to the querulous, bald-headed old boozer who had once been Rifleman Dodd.

CHAPTER TWENTY-TWO

Dodd's mates greeted him with laughter when they recognized him; he joined his section bashfully enough, at Captain Fotheringham's orders. Rifleman Barret, the company wit, promptly labelled him 'the King of the Cannibal Islands', a nickname which was much approved. They could afford to jest; they had just spent a winter in comfortable cantonments, and every man was well-fed and properly clad, in startling contrast with the bare-footed, naked multitude of living skeletons which Dodd had been harassing. And they were in high spirits too. The Army knew, even if England yet did not, that the tide of the war had turned. All the unembarrassed might of the French Empire had fallen before them, and not merely the French army but the French system—the new terrible style of making war which had overrun Europe for nineteen years—had failed.

When the bugles blew and the men fell in to resume the advance they did so lightheartedly. They were marching forward, and the French were falling back before them in ruin. They could guess at the triumphs yet to come, even though the great names of Salamanca and Vittoria were still hidden in the future. There was exhilaration in the ranks, and jests flew backwards and forwards as they marched. As for Dodd, he might as well have been in heaven. He was back in the regiment, in the old atmosphere of comradeship and good-fellowship. Up at the head of the line the bugle band was blowing away lustily with half the buglers, as ever, blowing horribly flat. The very dust of the road and the smell of the sweating ranks were like the scent of paradise. The tread of marching feet and the click of accoutrements were like the harps and cymbals. He tramped along with them in a dreamy ecstasy.

At the allotted camping ground the Portuguese guard turned out and presented arms; they were saluting the Ninety-Fifth; there was no thought of saluting the man who had just returned from an adventure calling for as much courage and resolution and initiative as any that the regimental history could boast. Dodd would have scoffed at any such idea. He was looking forward to his bread ration; he was hungry for bread. And there would be salt too; it was weeks since he had tasted salt—there had been none with which to savour the stinking mule meat of his recent meals. And there would be a go of brandy, too, with any luck.

As he sat and munched, warming himself deliciously at the fire, his eye caught the sight of a twinkling point of light far away on a hill-top, beyond the lines of the English fires. He did not think twice about it; it might be the fire of a French outpost or of a party of irregulars.

Actually, it had been lighted by irregulars; in it they were burning Sergeant Godinot to death. Dodd did not know. He did not know there had been such a man as Sergeant Godinot. What he did know was that he had borrowed an extra lot of salt from Eccles. He dipped his bread in it luxuriously, and munched and munched and munched.

We hope you have enjoyed this Large Print book. Other Chivers Press or Thorndike Press Large Print books are available at your library or directly from the publishers.

For more information about current and forthcoming titles, please call or write, without obligation, to:

Chivers Large Print
published by BBC Audiobooks Ltd
St James House, The Square
Lower Bristol Road
Bath BA2 3BH
UK
email: bbcaudiobooks@bbc.co.uk
www.bbcaudiobooks.co.uk

OR

Thorndike Press
295 Kennedy Memorial Drive
Waterville
Maine 04901
USA
www.gale.com/thorndike
www.gale.com/wheeler

All our Large Print titles are designed for easy reading, and all our books are made to last.